THE PRIVATE THOUGHTS OF
AMELIA E. RYE

THE PRIVATE THOUGHTS OF
AMELIA E. RYE

Bonnie Shimko

Farrar Straus Giroux / New York

For Bob

Copyright © 2010 by Bonnie Shimko
All rights reserved
Distributed in Canada by D&M Publishers, Inc.
Printed in March 2010 in the United States of America
by RR Donnelley & Sons Company, Harrisonburg, Virginia
Designed by Robbin Gourley
First edition, 2010
1   3   5   7   9   10   8   6   4   2

www.fsgkidsbooks.com

Library of Congress Cataloging-in-Publication Data
Shimko, Bonnie.
The private thoughts of Amelia E. Rye / Bonnie Shimko.— 1st ed.
    p.   cm.
Summary: Growing up in a small town in upstate New York during the 1960s,
a young girl, unwanted by her mother, searches for love and acceptance.
    ISBN: 978-0-374-36131-0
    [1. Family problems—Fiction.   2. Mothers and daughters—Fiction.
3. Friendship—Fiction.   4. New York (State)—History—20th century—Fiction.]
I. Title.

PZ7.S5566Pr 2010
[Fic]—dc22

                                                    2008048092

THE PRIVATE THOUGHTS OF
AMELIA E. RYE

WARNING!

This is a personal memoir. It is as private as a diary, but what I had to say would never have fit on those puny little pages, so I wrote it in book form like a real author, which I plan to be someday, unless I change to a hairdresser.

I can only hope that you are a considerate person and that you will close this book right now and put it back where you found it. If you insist on being nosy, don't believe everything you read. I am a very good liar. I curse, too, so if you are one of those goody-goody types, you might as well go put on something frilly and have a tea party. I wouldn't want you to get your squeaky-clean brain all messed up.

1

My mother tried to kill me before I was born. Even then I disappointed her.

I learned about the foundation of my life brick by brick from my daddy's daddy, Grandpa Thomas, and from Mama. Grandpa Thomas handed me the bricks gently, adding a fib or two to make our family seem halfway normal. Mama threw the bricks at me, aiming to kill. That woman had a mean streak in her as wide as the Atlantic Ocean.

My father grew up in a flea-size town in the upper right-hand corner of New York State, just up the road from Sullivan's Falls. Grandpa Thomas used to chuckle, "If your grandma Nellie'd birthed your daddy an inch farther to the north, he'd have been born speaking Canuck, eh?" I personally do not think it is polite to call Canadians *Canucks*, but Grandpa Thomas would never have hurt anybody's feelings on purpose, so maybe he thought it was a compliment.

The summer Daddy turned thirteen, the same age I am now, a traveling preacher named Brother Marvin set up a tent in the middle of Sullivan's Falls. He and his wife, Sister Catherine, filled the tent with folding chairs and then nailed flyers all over town, inviting the sinners of the area to come to their revival meeting to be saved.

Grandma Nellie must have thought the devil had her whole family by the tail because she paid extra for front-row seats. My daddy wrapped his legs around the rungs of his chair, ate the popcorn Sister Catherine hawked like one of those vendors at a baseball game, and waited for the show to start.

Sister Catherine was dressed for the weather in a flimsy skirt and a low-cut blouse. She sang hymns, played the cornet, and passed the collection plate. Brother Marvin preached the word of God with a performance that dazzled the audience.

Grandma Nellie was so filled with the Holy Spirit that she sank to her knees with her arms raised to heaven, shouting, "Hallelujah!" and dragged Grandpa Thomas down with her. At the same time, my daddy leaned forward to get a better look at Sister Catherine's you-know-whats. He hollered, "Thanks for the blessing, Lord!" then fell flat on his face with his legs still attached to that chair. Grandma Nellie thought Daddy'd been struck by a bolt of godliness. She was so overcome with gratitude that her entire family had been saved from the fires of hell that she put an extra quarter on the collection plate the next time it was passed. From then on, most everything my father thought was fun suddenly became a sin.

When Daddy graduated high school, Grandma Nellie gave him the choice of staying home to work the farm or being ordained by Brother Marvin the next time he came to town. Daddy hated cows and the mess that went along with them, so he chose religion. I guess he figured when *he* was a bona fide preacher, that list of sins would get a whole lot shorter.

According to Brother Marvin, the most important thing a preacher needs is a wife, preferably a musical beauty like Sister Catherine, to loosen up the tightwads. That's where Mama came in. Daddy wasn't crazy about her thick glasses and her even thicker ankles, but he did like the fact that she could play the piano and, better yet, that her parents had died and left her a three-bedroom bungalow on Navigation Street, complete with a detached garage and an almost-new Model T Ford. Besides, she was the best he could find. I guess he figured he could use his own good looks on the ladies of the congregation—let them convince their husbands to dig deep in their pockets to save their souls.

Mama was working as a waitress behind the luncheonette counter at Woolworth's. Daddy stopped in for Cokes and made her blush with his compliments about her charm and beauty. One day he asked her to have supper with him. She said she'd love to. He said, "Great! What time will it be ready?"

Mama's skill in the kitchen was the clincher. Daddy asked her to marry him, and they settled down on Navigation Street to begin their life together and start a family. Lucky for them, the preacher of the First Redeemer Church got fired because he was caught pocketing the special collection for poor little orphans. Daddy heard the good news, grabbed his spanking-new preacher certificate, rushed over to the church, and landed the job—just like that.

Thirty years passed before I showed up in Mama's belly. By then, my sister Sylvia was twenty-nine, married, and the mother of my four-year-old nephew, William. She lived in Maine and worked at the slipper factory. She was allowed to take her mistakes home, and she sent some to Mama and Daddy, so they wore slippers with the word REJECT stamped on them. My sister Charlotte was twenty-one. She thought the radio was talking to her through the radiator, and she heard strange voices coming from the walls, so she lived in the state mental hospital. And my nineteen-year-old brother, Jack? He was in Dannemora Prison, doing time for driving the getaway car in an armed robbery.

When I was inside my mother, she thought that I was a tumor and that all doctors were idiots, so she got into bed and waited to die. She soothed her upset stomach with Pepto-Bismol and watched her belly grow. One morning, the tumor kicked so hard that Mama's nightgown flew straight up in the air. When she realized what was happening, she went down to the kitchen, put the coffeepot on the stove, and punched my daddy so hard on his left ear that he had to go to the doctor to get it sewn up. Then Mama went back upstairs and took a flying leap out the window. When she landed headfirst in the barberry hedge, she was pure furious that I kept on kicking. And she blamed me for the scars on her face, too. The way I figure it, somebody as nearsighted as she was ought to put a little more planning into a project if she wants it to turn out right.

When Mama got even meaner, Daddy took off. That woman never missed a chance to tell me how it was my fault that her husband left Sullivan's Falls with Margo LaRue, the town hussy—in her brand-new, canary yellow Studebaker Champion bullet nose—at high noon, so everybody in town could witness the spectacle.

I had seen my daddy's picture, and he looked nice. I only wished he'd waited a few weeks and taken me with him. But if he'd stayed around any longer, Mama probably would have tried to kill him, too. Sometimes I sat by the window in my bedroom and watched for him. I just knew that he'd come back for me—soon, I hoped.

2

March 3, 1952. Welcome to the world,
Amelia Earhart Rye!

As soon as Daddy left, Mama phoned Grandpa Thomas to let him know what a snake his son had turned out to be. Then she informed him that unless he was willing to help raise this baby, she was going to leave me at the hospital to be put up for adoption.

By then, Grandma Nellie'd passed on. Grandpa Thomas had given up drinking but taken up gambling to fill the empty hours. Mama didn't know that he'd just lost the farm in a poker game and was about to be evicted. He wasn't crazy about the idea of sleeping under a bridge for the rest of his life, so he thought fast and said indignant-like, "No Rye baby has ever been brought up by strangers. It would be sacrilegious to let a thing like that happen." Then he paused for a long time and gave a loud sigh to make Mama think that he was trying to come up with a solution. "I guess I can put my life on hold for a while to help you out." Before Mama realized that she was having a big fat one put over on her, Grandpa Thomas had already moved in. And to sweeten the deal, he brought the brand-new RCA Victor twenty-one-inch "Super Set" TV he'd won in a raffle at the Clinton County Fair.

But things worked out different from what everyone expected. From the moment I was born, Grandpa Thomas wouldn't let me out of his sight. His tender heart surprised even him. "I didn't know so much love could come attached to one soggy little baby girl," he told me when I was old enough to understand. "When your daddy was born, your grandma thought I'd break him or dirty him up, so she kept him out of reach." He lowered his eyes and said, a little sheepish-like, "Course I was drinking a lot then, too." He gave me a big smooch on the forehead. "But I got a second chance when you came along."

Lucky for me, everybody in town had seen Grandpa Thomas passed out in the gutter a few times too many, so Mama was the one who had to go out and get a job, which she did not mind one little bit. According to her, working six days a week at the A&P, slicing bologna and Swiss cheese, was a whole lot better than being cooped up all day with a scruffy old man and a colicky kid.

Even though life was mostly just Grandpa Thomas

and me, by the time I was in school, Mama had managed to mess me up good. I don't blame her for passing on her bad eyesight or her mouse brown hair. But I do blame her for making me wear her old glasses, dressing me in my sisters' moth-eaten hand-me-downs that had sat in a trunk in the attic for twenty years, and cutting my hair with a do-it-yourself kit she saw advertised on TV. A girl dressed in World War I clothes and way-too-big glasses does not need a would-be Dutch boy haircut to finish it off. The rest of me is pretty much okay, more like my daddy's side of the family—tall and thin and regular-looking, plus china blue eyes.

I don't know who to blame for the counting, though. I guess just me. Not regular counting like in an arithmetic book. It was a dark kind where something in my head got stuck and made me do it. If I tried to ignore it, my heart thumped bad and I felt like I was being smothered and the nerves in my stomach tried to shake me apart. But when I went along with it, it took my mind away from what was happening.

If my teacher glared at me like I was a mistake of some kind because I couldn't read the word she'd written on the board, I'd make her disappear for a tiny minute.

One, two, three, four, five, six, seven.

"It's an easy one, Amelia," she'd say with a sigh. "You're just not trying."

One, two, three, four, five, six, seven.

When the biggest bully in the class stuck his foot into the aisle and laughed his head off when I fell and bloodied my nose, I'd get rid of him, too.

One, two, three, four, five, six, seven.

"Nice shoes, Pumpernickel," he'd say. "I hear antiques are worth a lot of money."

One, two, three, four, five, six, seven.

Counting kept me from crying while the snotty girls with the name-brand clothes and fake smiles said, "I love your glasses, Amelia. My grandmother had a pair just like those. They make your eyes look so big." Giggle, giggle. "And that's such a pretty dress. I've never seen one like it."

One, two, three, four, five, six, seven.

Even though our house was nearly a mile from school, I walked home. That way I didn't have to pretend the taunting on the bus didn't bother me, and I knew Grandpa Thomas would be in the kitchen, waiting. He was the only one in the world I could be around and not feel all twisted up inside. I could just be my own awkward self, without anybody keeping score.

When I was nearly home, I'd work up a good stream of tears, then run in the front door, blatting like a billy goat, ready to tell him how much I hated school and that a herd of elephants couldn't drag me back there. He'd sit me down at the table, wipe my face with the tail end of his handkerchief, and pour us each a glass of milk. And never once did he tell me to stop my blubbering or to grow a thicker skin the way my mother would have if she'd been home. Then Grandpa Thomas would reach for my hand and lead me into the living room. I'd sit next to him on the couch and mold myself to fit the curve of his scrawny, skeleton body that smelled like Old Spice. He'd put his arm around me, take my hand in his, and inspect the fingernails I'd bitten down to nubs.

"You know those kids are just acting the way they were raised," he'd say, cupping my chin in his hand. "Why I wouldn't be surprised if it was one of their mothers that tried to run me down when I was out by the mailbox this morning. You have to feel kind of sorry for people like that, the ones who go through life kicking and snarling at everybody else just to make themselves feel better."

By then, my bawling would have shifted to hiccuping and sniffling. "Tell me how I got my name, Grandpa Thomas," I'd say in a pathetic voice. I have always had an actress quality in me that I can call on whenever I want to. "Just one more time and I promise I'll never ask again."

"You must be tired of hearing about it by now," he'd tease. "You already know every little thing that happened. Why don't you just go ahead and tell me?"

I'd look up at him, knowing full well that he'd run into a burning building if I asked him to. "But it's more fun when it comes from you," I'd say in the whiny, singsong voice that made my mother so angry she'd give me a licking when I used it around her. Then I'd burrow into him even further and think how I'd like to stay there for the rest of my life.

He'd shake his head and say something about me being his special girl. Then, before he'd start, he'd smile the big smile that showed every one of the teeth he kept in that glass by his bed at night.

While he cleared his throat and shifted in his seat to get ready, I'd walk my fingers along the gigantic veins that ran down his hands like swollen purple rivers, push them in, then watch them pop up again. His skin was so thin I could lift it away from the bones below and fold it in half like tissue paper.

"All right then. Here goes," he'd say, play-pinching my cheek. "Once upon a time, a gorgeous little baby girl was born right here in Sullivan's Falls." He always started out like that. As if he was telling a fairy tale and I was Snow White herself—the really pretty one in the Walt Disney movie, not the dopey-looking loser in the coloring books.

Then it was my turn. "What was that little baby's name?" I'd act all serious, as if I had no idea who he was talking about.

"Well, that's just it. She didn't have one."

"Why not? How come her mama didn't name her?"

"I guess because that little baby was so beautiful she wanted to think about it, pick the perfect one. She didn't want to give a baby that special just any old name."

Even back then, when I was too young to know much, that part sounded fishy. Wouldn't you want to be prepared? So that when they handed you your baby, you could say "Hello, little whatever-its-name-is" and make it feel wanted? When Grandpa Thomas first told me the story, I asked him what Mama called me before I got my real name. He turned all fidgety and finally said that he remembered her calling me things like *sweetheart* and *honey*. But he is not a very good liar.

"Right," I'd say. "Then what happened?"

He'd give me a little squeeze and clear his throat again. "Finally, after a couple of weeks, the mean old grandpa got sick and tired of waiting for the mama to name that baby and he up and did it himself."

I'd look at him and laugh. "That was you, the mean old grandpa."

He'd nod and make a giddyup noise with his mouth. "That was me, all right. And I gave that baby a name anybody'd be proud to wear."

"Didn't the mama get mad? Didn't she want to name her own baby?" That part always made me feel empty inside, but the rest of the story made up for it.

"Well, she had her chance. Sometimes a person just has to take charge and get a thing done."

"So how come you named me Amelia Earhart Rye?"

He'd tilt my head up and look into my eyes so deeply it was as if he could see straight through to my soul. "Well, the Rye part was already in place. But Amelia Earhart was one of the most courageous women of all time. I knew that if you were to survive in this mean old world you'd have to be as brave as she was and I thought that having her name might give you a little head start."

"It hasn't worked yet," I'd say with a sigh. "The kids in school don't think I'm brave or they wouldn't tease me all the time." I'd gaze up at him and make my eyes look as pitiful as a cocker spaniel's. "Do you think I'll ever have any friends?"

Then Grandpa Thomas would scoot himself around sideways, take my hands in his, and hold me at arm's length. "Friends? Why, you're so likable, you'll have more friends than you know what to do with."

"But when?"

"Well now. You just have to give it some time. Let people get to know you."

I'd let all my breath out and sit there, looking as defeated as I felt. "They already know me and they hate my guts."

"That just means the right ones haven't come along

yet. Besides, all a person needs in life is one true friend."

It was always about that time when the back door would open and we'd hear Mama's footsteps on the kitchen linoleum. *One, two, three, four, five, six, seven. One, two, three, four, five, six, seven. One, two, three, four, five, six, seven.*

3

The year I met Fancy Nelson and grew a backbone

Grandpa Thomas was right. It wasn't long before the best friend anybody could ask for walked into my life. Like my grandfather always said, "You have to let things happen in their own good time."

Fourth grade turned out to be my charm year. I had sweet Miss Urbank for my teacher. Miss Urbank loved everybody. She wore pearl earrings and Blue Grass cologne, and she made me feel as if I was worth something. But the best part of the whole thing was that, right after Easter vacation, the only Negro kid I had ever seen in person moved to Sullivan's Falls. Her grandmother had been old Judge Watson's maid. When she died, her daughter came to take her place. And she brought my salvation with her.

"I'd like you to meet Frances Nelson," Miss Urbank

said after she'd ushered the new girl in the door and over to the front of the room. "She's moved here all the way from Alabama."

That girl was short and skinny and had the knobbiest knees I'd ever seen, but she stood in front of all those big-eyed kids, looked up at Miss Urbank, and then, in a loud voice, said, "I prefer to be called Fancy, ma'am. Frances is my church name and what my mama calls me when I drive her crazy, and I hate it. I just want everybody to know right now that I'll whop anybody good who calls me anything but Fancy." Then, in the sweetest tone you can imagine, she said, "I'll take that empty seat over by the window. I just love to watch the clouds float by, don't you?"

While every eye in that room watched Fancy Nelson strut over to the seat right next to mine, swinging her book bag to the beat of her steps, Miss Urbank smiled and said, "Well, yes, as a matter of fact, I do." Then she went back to the long division problems on the board as if that kind of thing happened every day—a colored girl walking into the room, threatening to pulverize everybody.

I loved that girl from the very start. And even though I didn't know him, except to see him drive down Main Street in his long black DeSoto automobile, I loved old Judge Watson for bringing her to Sullivan's Falls.

All of a sudden, I was old news and Fancy's brown skin and head full of braids and barrettes became the new target. At recess that first day, I sat by the fence with a book and watched as the kids waited until Miss Urbank was occupied on another part of the playground. Then, a few at a time, they'd circle Fancy like sharks, moving in for the kill. She'd plant her hands on her hips, lean her top half toward the tormentors, and waggle her head back and forth. I couldn't hear what she was saying, but whatever it was, it didn't take long till that group ran off and another took its place. Finally, Miss Urbank went over to see what was going on. She put her arm around Fancy's shoulder and brought her over to where I was sitting. I quick opened *The Hundred Dresses* and pretended that I was engrossed in the story and shouldn't be disturbed.

"Amelia, you and Fancy have something in common," Miss Urbank said as they reached the fence. She was out of breath, and her words sounded like the high notes on a violin.

Now what could I have in common with a colored girl who isn't afraid of anything? I wondered.

"You're both wearing red!"

She is really digging deep to find a similarity is what I thought. But I kept that to myself, and without looking up I said, "Oh, right."

"Well, why don't you two get acquainted while I go

back to the others?" Then Miss Urbank was off and I was there with a dry mouth and excitement skittering up and down my backbone.

Fancy knelt next to me, grabbed hold of her knees, and locked her elbows so her arms were as stiff as sticks. "What are you doing over here all by yourself?" she asked. "Don't you like to play?"

I kept my head down and pretended to read the book I'd found in our attic at home.

"Well? I asked you a question."

All of a sudden, Fancy's voice had turned into Mama's. *One, two, three, four, five, six, seven.*

"Aren't you going to answer me?"

I held up the book but didn't look at her. "I need to finish this. It's due today at the public library and I just started it." The lie drifted from my mouth as easy as breathing.

She reached for the book, thumbed through the pages, and mumbled under her breath, "This isn't even *from* the library. It belongs to some girl named Charlotte. Her name's written in the front."

I knew she was onto me, and I thought she was going to call me a liar and leave. Instead, she said, "I read this. It's really good. Teaches you not to stand by and watch people get messed with, to get busy and do something about it." Fancy looked around the playground, took in a huge breath, and shook her head. "I don't think any of *these* kids have read it. Want to go play now?"

Nobody'd ever asked me that before, so I jumped up fast, and as I followed her to the edge of the playground, I thought how her mother must really love her. Everything she had on was brand-new, even genuine penny loafers and kneesocks that matched her jumper—the expensive-looking kind with her initials sewn on the front. Fancy ran ahead and climbed to the top of the monkey bars. "Come on up," she called. "You can see the whole playground from here."

"I can't. I'm wearing a dress."

"Who cares? So am I," she shouted.

"But my underwear'll show and everybody'll make fun of me."

She shrugged her shoulders. "I have a feeling they do that already. That's why you were hiding, isn't it?"

She came right out with it. Didn't beat around the bush like most people would have. It was better that way. Got it over quick so I didn't have a case of nerves wondering when it would come. "Yeah, they have a good old time."

"Well, let's give 'em something more to talk about. I'll keep them busy while you get up here."

In a breath, she wrapped her legs around the top rung, threw herself backward, and hung by her knees. Her jumper covered her head, but the rest of her was a free-of-charge peep show. And the thing that surprised me most wasn't that her underpants were right there on display but that even her stomach was a smooth, golden brown—like maple syrup.

While I climbed to the top, Fancy didn't move, just hung there like a possum taking a nap.

"Okay, I'm up," I said.

The muscles in Fancy's legs balled up as she locked her feet under the corners of the bars and lifted herself upright. I looked across the playground at the gawking faces of the two worst bullies in the class, the Robertson twins, and a group of googly-eyed girls with their hands covering their mouths. "What'd you say to them that made them stay away?" I asked.

"Nothing much. Just that my daddy's crazy and he's got a gun and he shoots little brats that mess with his daughter."

My mouth fell open. "Your father has a gun?"

"I don't know. Maybe. I've never met him."

"Well, then how do you know he's crazy?"

She shrugged. "He must be. Anybody who'd leave my sweet, beautiful mama has to be nuts."

It looked like Fancy and I had more in common than red. And now that she was part of my life, those bullies and stuck-up girls didn't scare me as much. I thought maybe that imaginary gun would protect us both. Just to see, I wrapped my feet around the corners of the bars, threw myself backward, and let my sister's underpants shock the eyeballs out of those miserable kids. I waited for the teasing to start, but nobody said a word.

Fancy had brought some sort of magic with her that rubbed off on me. And Grandpa Thomas was right. All you need in life is one true friend.

4

Lies, blue eyes, and Margo LaRue

From then on, I wished I could spend every single second with Fancy, but asking her to come to my house would have been too risky. I wasn't worried about Grandpa Thomas. He'd swallow his tongue before he'd say anything that might embarrass me or hurt the friend I'd waited so long for. But Mama could recite scripture out one side of her mouth and spit venom out the other. She thought anybody that wasn't the same color as she was had broken the law and ought to be punished, so she stepped up and volunteered for the job. More than once, I'd heard her call Fancy's grandmother a—well, you know the word— and I would rather have eaten bugs than given her the chance to do that to Fancy.

The day we finished fourth grade and were leaving school for summer vacation, Fancy invited me to go to her house that coming Sunday. I said, *"Yes!"* before she had a chance to take a breath and add the staying for supper part. A little mouse thrill ran up the back of my neck when I pictured myself walking into old Judge Watson's house. It's big and ancient and dark. Just the thought of it was as delicious as the feeling I got while I watched monster movies at the Strand Theater on Saturday afternoons.

When I told Mama about my invitation, I rearranged the facts just the tiniest bit so she wouldn't throw a fit about me playing with a Negro girl. Even though I'd be at a rich white person's house, in Mama's lopsided brain, the colored thing would have contaminated it. Kind of like the gob of spit I used to add to her coffee after she'd tanned my hide.

"A girl asked me to go to her house on Sunday afternoon," I told Mama after I finished the supper dishes and she was all set up comfortable on the couch in front of the television set. *The Lawrence Welk Show* was about to start, which always put her in a good mood. That woman was crazy about accordion music—especially when Myron Floren played "Lady of Spain." The way she sat there, staring at him with big old cow eyes, it was as if she thought he'd dedicated it just to her.

"What girl?" Mama asked. She was stirring the cup of coffee I'd made her.

"Well—uh—her name is—um—Faith Divine!" That

was the churchiest thing I could come up with on short notice. In my mind, I smacked myself on the forehead. Why hadn't I thought up a name before I said anything? She'd never buy that one. Nobody'd call a kid anything that corny. Mama'd tell me to quit lying and send me to bed.

"Faith Divine," she sighed, all soupy-like. "I wish I'd given you a nice Bible name. I must have been crazy, letting your grandfather name you after that Earhart creature who thought she was a man."

I didn't care *what* Amelia Earhart thought she was. I was just glad that Grandpa Thomas had saved me from the fate of having to go through life with a name like Faith Divine.

"Does she go to school with you?" Mama was looking straight at me.

I hadn't thought about this one either, but I was surprised at how fast my brain worked. "She doesn't go to school." Mama never attended school events like regular parents, but I wasn't taking a chance that she might start and ask about my new friend Faith.

"What are you talking about? Kids *have* to go to school."

I got all sad-sounding. "She has to take care of her sick mother." That didn't sound like enough. "And Faith is crippled. She had polio, so she has to wear those big, heavy braces, poor thing."

Oh, for crying out loud. I should have rehearsed better. I lied to Mama all the time about little things, but this was big and important, and I was messing it up bad.

"Well, that's a shame," Mama said, in a sympathetic tone. "But she must still have to go to school. I don't—"

"Her mother used to be a teacher, so Faith has her lessons at home." I didn't even know where that came from, but I thought it was pretty good.

"You said that her mother was sick."

Oh, rats. I forgot about that part. "Well—she is, only she's just a little bit sick." By then, *I* was feeling more than a little bit sick myself.

"She sounds like a nice girl. But I've never even heard about the Divines. And how does Faith know you?"

Damn! This was way harder than I'd figured it would be. "They probably shop at the Grand Union, so that's why you haven't seen them." That sure was stupid. How are a mother who's too sick to take care of herself and a kid who can't walk going to shop anywhere?

Mama nodded as if that made sense. "But how do you know Faith?"

"I don't really know her yet. Her cousin goes to my school and she thinks Faith and I would get along with each other. So *she* asked me. Besides, they just moved here and I guess they like to keep to themselves—what with the crippled thing and all." Even *I* wouldn't have believed *that* one.

"Where does she live?" Mama asked, reaching for the jar of peanuts on the coffee table.

Well for goodness' sake. I could definitely win first place in a lying contest. Plus, I had this part all figured out good. "Over on Bartlett Street. Next to the library." Bartlett is one street down from Judge Watson's house. I thought putting the fake girl's house near Fancy's might save my skin if some big-mouth grocery shopper told Mama she'd seen me in the neighborhood.

"But that's way on the other side of town," Mama said around the mouthful of peanuts she was working on.

My insides got all smiley. Yes, it was. And it was far enough away so that she would never go there. Grandpa Thomas had lost his license when he backed his '49 Packard over a curb and flattened a parking meter, and Mama thought driving wasn't ladylike, so she sold the car when Daddy ran off with Margo LaRue and she walked the few blocks to work and church, the only places she ever went. "It's not that far," I said. "I can run it in ten or fifteen minutes."

Mama gave me a dirty look. "Girls don't run," she said, as if it was an actual written-down rule. "You'll walk like a civilized person."

That was it. The Lawrence Welk music started, and Mama was off to Polka Land. And in a few days, I'd be off to Fancy's house. The fun was about to begin!

When Sunday finally came, Mama made me wear my sister Charlotte's favorite dress ever—the pathetic salmon-colored one with the dumb daffodil pattern and the ladybug buttons down the front. I'd hidden it in the bottom of the trunk in the attic and was hoping I'd get so big that I'd never have to wear it, but no such luck. And if that wasn't bad enough, Mama got it into her head that an outfit that pretty needed a hair ribbon to finish it off—a great big floppy yellow thing with long streamers down the back. I looked like a gigantic two-year-old on her way to a birthday party.

Mama stood behind me in front of the mirror. "There," she said, all proud. "This will show that little crippled girl's mother that you're from a proper family and that I know how to dress you up nice for a visit."

I kept my mouth shut about how stupid I looked, because I knew if I told Mama what I thought, she'd swat the vinegar out of me and make me stay home. Sass made her boil over fast, so I did a lot of talking to her in my head instead of to her face. That way, I could keep my brain from exploding and still live.

On my way to Judge Watson's, I was about to untie the bow and shove it into the neighbor's hedge when the Robertson twins came around the corner on their bikes and nearly plowed me down. They'd already repeated a grade and were a head taller than me. My first thought was to run, but I was so frozen with fear, I couldn't move. Then the boys got off their bikes and corralled me.

"Well, looky here," Jake said, in a fake girlie voice. "Looks like Rye's all gussied up for her sweetie."

"You got a sweetie, Rye?" Eddie taunted.

I didn't answer, just kept counting to seven in my head. And then my kneecaps started to dance. That's what happens when I get *really* scared. I don't shake or turn white like most people. My kneecaps do calisthenics and try to push themselves straight through my skin.

Jake rolled his front tire onto one of the ugly Mary Jane shoes Mama made me wear. They were way too big, so she'd stuffed the toes with toilet paper and I didn't feel that tire at all. When I didn't react, Jake backed up and asked in his usual smart-ass voice, "Who'd have her for a sweetie anyway?"

"I guess she's just out looking for one," Eddie added. "She ought to try the dog pound."

Jake seemed to think that was the funniest thing he'd ever heard. "Yeah," he said. "She ought to try the dog pound."

"Speaking of dogs," Eddie said, "Ma likes to put ribbons on our basset hound." He reached over and yanked the bow off my head. Some strands of hair came with it. "Sparkles'll look a lot better with this than Rye here."

That threw both twins into a laughing fit. Then Eddie noticed the hair in the ribbon and that my eyes had teared up. "What's the matter, Rye?" he said in a singsong voice. "Did I hurt your tender little head?"

My head hardly hurt at all, but when I thought about what they might do next, I really started to cry. Big fat blubbering sobs came out of me.

I guess the twins figured they'd done enough because they got back on their bikes. As they rode away, Jake yelled, "Hey, Rye. It was fun chewin' the fat with you. We'll have to do it again soon."

Jake and Eddie had teased me before, but always from across the street or when they passed me in the crowded halls at school. They'd never cornered me alone. As soon as they were out of sight, I wiped my face with the skirt of my dress and started walking again—fast. Then I broke into a sprint.

When I got to Fancy's house, my heart was pounding like crazy. Fancy was waiting for me on the front porch steps in jeans and a T-shirt like any normal person. "Well, don't you look adorable," she said, smiling. "Your mother sure does love to torture you."

Fancy knew about my train-wreck family. And I knew how she'd been tormented so bad in Alabama that Sullivan's Falls seemed friendly. She patted the spot next to her on the step, smiled, and said, "Sit down. It's nice out." And then she added, "What'd you do, run all the way over here? You're panting like a racehorse."

I sat extra close to her, and while I was catching my breath, I told her about the Robertson twins. But I didn't tell her how scared I was or that I'd bawled like a baby. I knew *she* never would have cried like that.

"They're such jerks," she said. "I guess they don't have anything better to do."

Just being with Fancy made me feel stronger, and I was beginning to breathe normal again. "Well, I was a perfect target in this getup. I probably would have made fun of me, too."

Fancy laughed, grabbed my hand, and turned toward the front door. "Come on. I want you to meet my mother."

The inside of the house was a big fat disappointment. It wasn't one bit scary. The living room was decorated pretty in bright colors with lady wallpaper and brand-new furniture—Danish modern like in the magazines.

"This isn't what I expected," I said.

"What isn't?" Fancy asked, as she plopped down on a lemon yellow sofa with smooth wooden arms that matched the coffee table. Then she pulled me down next to her.

"Well, it's such an old house; I thought it would be dark and spooky inside, too."

My eyes about fell out of my head as I watched Fancy plant the toes of her sneakers on the edge of the coffee table. My mother would have killed me if I tried that at home, even with our old, beat-up stuff. "I guess it used to be kind of spooky," she said. "But before we moved here, the judge had it all done over, except for his room. My grandmother must have told him that Mama's real good at keeping a house nice. So when Granny died and he asked us to come, I suppose he wanted to make sure Mama wouldn't leave when she saw this place."

"Is he here?" I asked, hoping she'd say no. I certainly wouldn't know what to say to a judge.

"Yeah, he's here," she said, as if she was talking about her pet goldfish instead of the most important person in town. "But mostly he stays in his room. And if you want to see spooky, that's the place to go, except I'm not allowed in there." Then she smiled, sly. "Unless my mother's occupied and he's at work."

Things were starting to get a little bit interesting. "Oh, and I'm sorry about your grandmother," I said, just because I thought I should.

"What are you sorry about? You didn't do anything." Her matter-of-fact voice surprised me. "Besides, I never knew her. She lived here years ago, when she was young. But then she moved to Alabama for a while. That's where my mother was born." Fancy shook her head. "I don't think Granny was a very good mother because she left my mama in Alabama with my great-grandma and she came back here to work for the judge. Then she up and died before I could meet her—just got out of bed one morning and keeled over. Stone dead before she hit the floor—heart attack."

I couldn't imagine how a mother could just leave her baby so far away like that. "That's terrible," I said. "I'm really sorry."

"It's okay. When my mama said that Granny had passed on, it was like she was talking about some old famous person. I didn't feel anything. I tried to act sad, but I'm no good at pretending."

I will have to give her some lessons is what I was thinking when I heard footsteps in the hall.

"I thought somebody was in here," a sweet voice said. The words were drawn out and curvy, the same way Fancy talked. And Fancy was right. Her mother *was* beautiful. Like *Leave It to Beaver*'s mother, only with light brown skin and short black hair and eyes as blue as mine. She was wearing the same style dress as Mrs. Cleaver, though, and even had on high heels— light green leather with smashed-down bows.

"It's just us, Mom," Fancy said. She left her feet on the table and her mother did not say one single thing about it. Didn't yell or anything. When she leaned down and gave Fancy a kiss on the cheek, a pang of jealousy bit my heart.

"And you must be Amelia," Mrs. Nelson said, holding out her hand in my direction. "I'm happy to meet you." Her fingernails were all done up medium pink to match her lipstick—plain, not the frosted kind that floozies wear.

I had never shaken hands with anybody before, so I just sat there like a dunce until my brain woke up and told me to stick mine out. Instead of saying something polite like "I'm happy to meet you, too," I giggled and nodded my head. Sometimes I am just plain hopeless.

"Well, why don't you girls go up to Fancy's room and have fun," Mrs. Nelson said, smiling at me. "I have some letters to write. I'll bring you a snack when I'm finished." The way Fancy's mother treated me like a real person caught me off guard. Sometimes you do not know what you are missing until it hits you smack in the face.

Once in a while a thing surprises you so much that your heart does a somersault—like when I walked into Fancy's bedroom. It looked as if Elizabeth Taylor had it decorated in movie-star style for *her* daughter—thick, rose-colored carpet and even a white canopy bed with one of those lacy tops. Then I saw it—a genuine Princess telephone right there on her nightstand. The only place I'd ever seen one of those was in ads in *McCall's* magazines at the drugstore. Rich teenagers and modern mothers owned them, not ten-year-old girls.

"Does this thing work?" I asked, petting the smooth, pink plastic, then running my fingers over the round dial plate.

"Yeah, it works," Fancy answered. "Try it if you want to." She was rummaging through a pile of games on a table by the window.

I pulled my hand away from the phone. It was as if she'd just given me permission to drive Judge Watson's car. "Who would I call?"

"I don't know. Anybody you want to. Call Paris, France, if you feel like it. The judge won't care."

Grandpa Thomas played cards on Sunday, and I certainly wasn't going to call Mama. She'd bawl me out for bothering her and tell me if this was the kind of shenanigans I was up to I should get myself on home and she'd find something better for me to do with my time. "That's okay," I said. "I was just wondering if it worked." I looked over at Fancy. "Who do you call?"

"Nobody." Now she was searching her closet shelf.

"Then how come you have a phone?"

She shrugged. "It was here when I came. Along with all this other stuff."

Something else surprised me. She had a night-light in every single light socket. I pointed to one. "What are all those for?" I asked. "Don't you like the dark?"

She didn't answer right away, but then she said, "They were there when we moved in." She moved a pile of books and reached behind them. "Oh, here it is!" she said.

"Here what is?"

"My Magic 8 Ball. I love to fool around with this thing."

I'd never seen a Magic 8 Ball before, but it looked interesting. "What do you do with it?"

"You ask it questions. It's like a little fortune-teller."

"Yeah, *right*," I said. "That black ball's going to tell us our future?"

"Yup. Come on over by the window. We can see the answers better."

When Fancy and I got settled on the carpet, she held up the ball and shook it. "I'll go first so you can see how it works," she said with importance in her voice. "Um—let's see. Okay, here goes. Are we having chicken for supper?" She gave it another shake, then turned it over. "It says 'Don't count on it.' It's right! We're having roast beef. Now it's your turn."

She handed it to me, and even though I knew it was just a toy, I was willing to give it a try. "Do I have to say my questions out loud?" I asked Fancy.

"Not if you don't want to."

"All right, then. I'll do it." In my head, I asked the question I asked myself every day. *Is my father coming back for me?* I shook the ball and waited for the answer. "Reply hazy, try again" appeared in the little window on the bottom.

"Do it!" Fancy said.

I took a deep breath, shook the ball, and in my mind repeated *Is my father coming back for me?* The ball answered "Better not to tell you now."

"This is dumb," I mumbled. I was starting to feel creepy about the whole thing. I knew that ball wasn't magic, but I didn't want it to tell me that my daddy didn't care.

"Try a different question," Fancy said. "It's really fun once you get going."

"Okay." I sighed. "Just one more and then let's do something else." I thought for a moment. "Is my mother as mean as a skunk?" I said out loud. "Yes— Definitely."

"See? I told you!" Fancy giggled. "You just had to get it warmed up."

Okay, I thought. *Maybe the ball did work.* I went back to my daddy, but I chose a safer question. *Does anybody know where my father is?* "You may rely on it." My heart started to pound as I shook the ball. I could hardly wait for the answer to my next question. *Will I be able to ask that person about him?* "It is certain." I was so excited I could barely breathe. *Does that person live in Sullivan's Falls?* "Concentrate and ask again." But I didn't have to ask the ball again, because right that very minute, a beat-up canary yellow Studebaker Champion bullet nose pulled into the driveway across the street.

I couldn't believe it. I'd never seen a bullet nose in real life—only in Grandpa Thomas's *Car and Driver* magazines. He was an expert on cars, and he'd passed everything he knew down to me. And that Studebaker even had the chrome luggage rack on the top—an accessory that cost extra—like the one that held my daddy's suitcases when that tramp Margo LaRue drove him out of my life. Was that her? Had she come back? Suddenly, I felt dizzy. I pointed to the woman getting out of the car. "Do you know who that is?" I asked Fancy.

"She moved in there a few weeks ago," Fancy said. "Her name's Margo. Margo LaRue."

My insides went wild and I couldn't take a full breath. Finally, I calmed down enough to ask, "Does she own that house? It's huge."

"No, she rents a room on the top floor. She's an Avon Lady and she works at Jackson's Funeral Home, doing the books or something."

I wondered if the owners of the house knew how evil she was. They must not have or they'd've never let her on their property.

As I watched Margo LaRue walk toward the front door, I asked Fancy the only question that mattered.

"Does anybody live with her? I mean does she have a husband or anything?" I thought my heart would bust its way straight through my chest.

Fancy thought for a moment. "Nah. She's all by herself. She looks kind of weird because of all the makeup she wears, but she's okay. When she comes to sell my mother Avon stuff, she lets me try it on, and gives me samples of all kinds of goop. She's nice."

When Fancy said that father-stealing hussy was *nice*, my stomach knotted up again. "*Nice* isn't the word I'd use," I said, angry.

"What do you mean? How do you even know her?"

"I don't really know her, but I know what she did, and so do you."

"I do?" Fancy looked at me as if I should go live with my sister Charlotte in the mental hospital. "What are you talking about?"

"Remember the woman I told you about who ran away with my father?"

Fancy opened her eyes wide. "You're kidding! She's the one?"

"Yup," I said, as disgusted as I felt.

Fancy stayed stone silent as I thought about what had just happened.

"I need to come up with a way to talk to her, find out where he is," I said. I thought about it some more. "And no matter what, she can't know who I am or she'll clam up."

By the time Mrs. Nelson came up to Fancy's room, holding a tray with two glasses of milk and a plate of cookies, we had everything figured out. "I hope you like peanut butter, Amelia," she said. "I made them this morning."

"I love peanut butter cookies, Mrs. Nelson," I said. "They're my favorite." That wasn't exactly true. I like date-filled sugar cookies best, but I thought I should be polite.

"Mom?" Fancy said.

"What, sweetie?"

"When's Miss LaRue going to deliver your Avon order?"

"I'm not sure. Why?"

"I was just wondering if Amelia can be here when she comes. She wants to buy her mother some perfume for her birthday."

"Of course," Fancy's mom said. "That's very thoughtful of you, Amelia. Which scent does she like?"

Mama never used perfume and I didn't know anything about Avon stuff or what it smelled like, so I blurted out the first thing that came to my mind. "I'm not sure what it's called, but the box it comes in has pink flowers on it."

"Oh!" Mrs. Nelson said. "You must mean To A Wild Rose. That's my favorite, too."

Sometimes you just luck out with a thing. "That's

the one!" I said, all fake excited. Then I thought how I'd need some time with Margo LaRue, and if I already knew what I wanted—well, that wouldn't be any good. "But I bet she'd like something different this time," I said fast. "Do you think Miss LaRue would let me sample some of the perfumes? I mean even though I'm just a kid?"

Mrs. Nelson laughed. "Well, you're a customer, and I know Margo won't mind if you take your time. Besides, she loves kids. She told me that she'd always wanted some of her own but she was never lucky that way."

Well, for goodness' sake. It never even dawned on me that I might have had little brothers and sisters running around.

"Thanks, Mrs. Nelson," I said. "Sounds like fun." And when she gave me my milk, I made sure my hand touched hers—the way I thought a daughter would touch her mother's hand.

"No problem, Amelia. Enjoy your snack. I'm going to go get dinner started."

"Do you need any help?" I asked, hoping she'd say yes. I felt bad about lying to her and I wanted to make up for it.

"No, thanks," she said, smiling. "But it's sweet of you to offer. You two have a good time and I'll call you when it's ready."

Mrs. Nelson's cookies weren't anywhere near as

good as what I was used to. I have to give Mama that much. That woman sure could cook, and she put her whole heart into it. I think it was the one thing that made her feel as if she was worth something.

When I got home from Fancy's, Mama was waiting for me in the kitchen with concerned eyes. I thought she was going to lay into me about not getting home in time to do the dishes, but she put her hand on my shoulder, soft like a whisper, and told me to sit down. The inside of my head went black. Something terrible must have happened. I'd never seen her like that before. The only thing I could think of was that my daddy was dead and I hadn't even had a chance to meet him yet. When Mama took hold of my hand, I got really scared. "What, Mama?" I said. "What is it?"

She looked at me with a kindness I didn't even know she was capable of showing. "It's your grandfather," she said in a soft voice. "He's in the hospital. He's had a heart attack."

It was as if all my air had been sucked out and I couldn't get any more in.

"They're not sure if he's going to pull through," Mama added. "We'll know more tomorrow."

Mama said other things while she was putting me to bed, but I don't remember what they were. All I could think was that, if Grandpa Thomas died, I would have to figure out some way to go with him.

5

Moldy bread, applesauce, and a hint of Grandpa Thomas

*G*randpa Thomas didn't die. And he didn't have a heart attack. Something in his brain busted open and left him motionless and unable to speak. Sick people made Mama nervous, so she wouldn't go near him. But as soon as he was moved out of the hospital and into Shady Oaks, the nursing home run by the county for people who don't have much money, I could walk over and visit him any time I wanted to.

The first time I went there, he was in a dark green La-Z-Boy in the corner of the sunroom, somber as a shadow. I sat on the arm of his chair, laid my head on his shoulder, and took hold of his hand. I kept my back to the other people in the room so I could pretend everything was like it used to be, and we were home on the couch in the living room—a family again. But instead of Old Spice, Grandpa Thomas smelled like moldy bread. And instead of a glass of milk, there was a half-finished jar of baby applesauce on the table next to him. He stared straight ahead, blinking once in a while, but said nothing. His silence let me imagine what he'd say if he could talk.

"We had hot dogs for lunch today," I said, examining the patch of whiskers below his ear that they'd missed when they shaved him.

That's great. You love hot dogs!

"Yup, and what did you have?" I tried not to look at that applesauce jar.

Well, now. Let's see. First off, I started with a big bowl of corn chowder, the kind with lots of potatoes and onions. Then a roast beef sandwich on wheat that was so thick, I could hardly get my mouth around it. And a nice cold bottle of beer—Molson.

"A Molson? Really?" Grandpa Thomas had told me lots of times how much he missed having an ice-cold beer, especially on a hot summer day. But I guess he knew that even one sip could send him back down the wrong path, so he didn't give in.

I can have a Molson any day I please. And as much as I want, because I never get drunk anymore.

I sat up and looked straight at him. "Maybe you'll get your driver's license back." I noticed for the first time that he had green specks in his velvety brown eyes—clear eyes like you see on a much younger person.

You're right. And then I'll buy one of those new Cad-dies that can do zero to sixty in ten seconds.

"The '62 powder blue Eldorado with the rocket fins we saw in the dealer's window?"

That's the one! I wiped drool that was traveling down his chin with the edge of the giant bib they had tied around his neck. I wanted to rip that thing off and tell the jerk who'd put it there what she could do with it. But I also wanted to be able to come back, so I behaved myself.

I got tired of discussing cars, so I brought up what I really wanted to talk to him about. "You weren't home, so I couldn't tell you about my visit to Fancy's house."

I was wondering about that. Did you have a good time?

"It was all right," I said, in an absentminded kind of way. The fun I'd had at Fancy's was so muddied up by what happened to Grandpa Thomas that I didn't know how I felt.

Just all right? I thought you'd have the time of your life.

Since Grandpa Thomas was still alive, my mind must have decided that it was okay to relax and remember the good part of that awful day. "I had a great time," I said in a cheery voice. "After supper, I rode Fancy's bike, and she even let me try her new pogo stick." I didn't add the part about me falling off that thing and breaking my front tooth, because Grandpa Thomas worried about stuff like that. Mama didn't. She just got mad. When she found out that Grandpa Thomas wasn't going to die, she bawled me out good and told me to file the sharp, pointy part of the tooth with an emery board. I guess she wasn't about to spend perfectly good money taking me to a dentist after I did something that stupid. And it didn't really matter that my teeth didn't match. It blended in better on me than it would have on a perfect girl. Besides, I didn't smile that much anyway.

I couldn't think of any more things for Grandpa Thomas to ask me, so I fiddled with the veins on his hand until I worked up the courage to bring up Margo LaRue. "Daddy's girlfriend's back," I finally said straight out. I figured that might make him so mad he'd snap out of whatever state he was in. But no, just more imaginings in my head.

You mean to tell me that jezebel has the gall to show her face in this town?

The way she was dressed, she was showing the town a whole lot more than her face. "She lives right across from Fancy," I said. "I'm going to see her tomorrow. I'll try to find out where Daddy is."

Good idea. And when you do, let me know. I'd like to tell that son of mine what I think of the stunt he pulled.

I looked at Grandpa Thomas's watch. "It's getting late. I have to go. But there's just one more thing I want to ask you."

What's that?

"Do you think my daddy will ever come back for me?"

I waited. Nothing from him but a tiny sigh. I laid my head back down on his shoulder. Tears burned my eyes and sadness surrounded me like fog.

6

*Sometimes when you want to hate
a person, your stubborn little heart
gets in the way.*

The Avon Lady's here!" Fancy said as she hurried into the kitchen. "My mother's paying for her order and then we get old Floozie LaRuezie all to ourselves. Mama said I can order something, too. And I'll take my time picking it out so you can ask her all the questions you want."

"Oh. Okay," I said. Maybe the whole thing wasn't such a great idea after all. A huge family of butterflies had moved into my stomach, and it felt as if they were having a shindig. I'd folded my three dollar bills—the money Grandpa Thomas gave me for Christmas—so many times they were barely the size of postage stamps. I shoved them in my pocket and started biting my fingernails.

Fancy sat at the kitchen table right next to me and said, "Wait till you see the getup she has on. Her blouse has one of those cutout fronts that shows almost everything she's got. Plus, if she bends over in that skirt, we're gonna see a full moon in the middle of the day." Fancy made her eyebrows do push-ups. "And guess what?"

"What?"

"This morning, I overheard the cleaning lady tell my mother what Miss LaRue does at Jackson's Funeral Home. It's not balancing the books." Fancy had a sly look on her face, and the sparks in her eyes told me that something juicy was coming.

"What does she do?" I asked. I could hardly stand the suspense.

Fancy leaned in close and whispered, as if she were telling me top secret information. "Hair. And makeup."

The excitement drained clear out of me. I just hate it when you are expecting something good and then— nothing. "Whose hair and makeup? Mr. Jackson's wife?" Back then, I did not know very much.

Fancy looked at me as if I was the biggest moron she'd ever come across. "His customers!" She stuck her finger in her mouth and made a gigantic gagging noise. "Can you imagine?"

"No! You mean she actually touches dead people?"

"Yup. Even shampoos their hair and puts it up on rollers."

"Eeewww!" Just the thought of it sent shivers up and down my arms. "That's disgusting."

"But I guess she's really good at her job," Fancy said. "According to the cleaning lady, she uses her Avon products on the stiffs, and they look better than they did when they were alive. In fact, a lot of women go to wakes of people they don't even know just to get a peek at the new line of cosmetics and a whiff of the latest colognes—so they can look and smell as good as the dead woman in the casket."

"You're making this up," I said, impatient.

"No, I'm *not*."

I'd never heard Fancy lie before, but what she'd just said couldn't possibly be true. And something else confused me. "Why do you have a cleaning lady?" I asked. "I thought your mother took care of the house."

"That's what everybody thinks, but really all she does is the cooking and answers the phone—stuff like that."

"What about groceries? She must have to buy those." I hadn't thought about Mrs. Nelson going to the A&P, meeting Mama, and spilling the beans about Fancy and me.

"All that stuff gets delivered. Besides, Mama mostly stays home. I guess it's better that way." Fancy's look turned a little sad. "She's not exactly on anybody's best-friends list. And she seems happy here. She likes to read and work in her garden. The judge takes real good care of her."

Something didn't smell right about Fancy's mother and Judge Watson, but I had no time to think about it because as soon as Margo LaRue walked into the kitchen and settled herself in the chair across from mine, my heart started doing jumping jacks. "And who's this pretty girl?" she said, looking straight at me.

"This is my friend Amelia," Fancy said fast—no last name, like we'd practiced. "She wasn't born in Sullivan's Falls or anything like that. She moved here a few years ago. Her father's in the army, so he's hardly ever home, but she *does* have one, and he's crazy about her."

Then it was my turn, but the pretty-girl thing had startled me so much that I forgot my line. When Fancy realized I wasn't going to be any help, she said, "Amelia's never met a real live Avon Lady before, so she's excited to be here. She wants to buy her mother some perfume, but can I try on some makeup first? My mother said I can buy something so I can play movie star—I just don't know what I want. And Amelia'd like to try some, too." She looked at me. "Right, Amelia?"

That was a surprise to me. Trying on makeup was at

the bottom of my list of things I wanted to do, but that woman had information about my daddy and I was going to get it out of her, even if I had to put goop on my face to do it. "Sure," I said. "Sounds like fun!"

"Well, aren't you just the sweetest little thing," Margo LaRue chirped at me. She reached across the table and patted my hand. Her fingernails were long and polished perfectly—bright red.

It is very confusing when you hate somebody so bad that you could spit tacks, and then they go and treat you special and tell you that you are pretty.

Mrs. Nelson stuck her head in the door and said, "I'm going upstairs now. If you need anything, just give a holler." She winked at Margo LaRue. "And, girls, have fun making your choices."

After Fancy's mother left, Margo LaRue said, "I don't have any little girls of my own to fuss over, so I'm just tickled pink that Mrs. Nelson is letting me spend time with you." She rearranged her skirt, then adjusted the sunflower clip in her way-too-blond hair. "Okay, now let's see what we've got in here." She opened the big black case on the table in front of her. "The new fall line is in and it's very exciting—lots of deep, rich colors." I wondered whether a woman who dressed in pea green and neon yellow would know a rich color if it stepped up and introduced itself. "Let's start with the lipsticks," she said as she dumped a pile of tiny white samples in the middle of the kitchen table along with a hand mirror, a jar of Pond's cold cream, and a box of Kleenex. "Now, Fancy, you can go ahead and try some like I showed you the last time I was here," she said. Then she looked over at me. "Would you like me to help you, Amelia, or would you rather do it yourself?"

Part of me wanted to tell Margo LaRue that she could throw her stupid little lipstick samples straight into the trash and jump in after them. But there was another part of me that felt cozy around this no-good tramp of a woman who'd stolen my father and wrecked my life. "I've never tried lipstick on before," I said. "Maybe you should help me."

"Well, sure, honey," she said, as if that's exactly what she'd been waiting to do her entire life. She slid her chair around to my side of the table and sat real close. Her breath smelled like peppermint Life Savers, and the rest of her reminded me of the rosebushes in Fancy's back yard. And when she held my chin, her hand felt warm and soft, not like how Mama's hand felt on my bare thigh when she was giving me my comeuppance for something I did that got her riled, like forgetting to put the milk back in the refrigerator or letting the neighbor's cat in. Somehow, I couldn't imagine Margo LaRue smacking anybody. "Now make your lips go like this," she said, forming her own mouth into a loose pout.

I must have done it wrong because she ran her

hand down my cheek and said, "Now just relax, sweetheart. This isn't going to hurt one little bit."

And I did.

She reached for one of the samples. "With your coloring, a light pink should be just the ticket." She applied the lipstick so gently; it was as if my mouth was fragile and she didn't want to break it. Then she folded a Kleenex in half, held it to my lips, and told me to kiss it. I'd never kissed anything before, but I knew what she meant, because I'd seen women do it in movies. "I was right," she said. "This one's perfect for you." She handed me the mirror. "What do you think?"

There was hardly anything to see, just a tiny bit of color—as if I'd eaten a cherry Popsicle.

"How about *this*?" Fancy said, elbowing me in the arm. "Don't I look beeeuteeful?" She puckered her blazing orange lips, bobbed her head back and forth, and fluttered her eyelashes.

I was so dazzled by the attention I was getting from Margo LaRue, I'd forgotten that Fancy was even there. "It looks good," I lied.

Then Margo LaRue laughed. "You look as if you lost a fight with a pumpkin." A sense of humor was the last thing I expected a woman like her to have. She stood up, grabbed a Kleenex, and reached over me. "And, precious, try to keep the lipstick on your mouth," she said to Fancy. "It doesn't belong on your chin."

"Let's try the eye shadow next," Fancy said as soon as she was cleaned up. "Wait till you see all the colors, Amelia."

As Margo LaRue rummaged around in the black case, Fancy caught my eye and mouthed, "Ask about your father."

I'd thought it was going to be so easy. Just throw out a few questions and the mystery would be solved. But now, all the rage and the courage I had built up were gone. And for some strange reason, I wanted to impress this woman, not pump her for information and then give her a piece of my mind like I had planned.

When Margo LaRue sat back down, I smiled at her. "Have you always been an Avon Lady?" That was the only thing I could think of.

"Well, not always. For about the last ten years though."

"Fancy said you just moved here. Where did you live before?" I tried to sound as if I was asking if she thought it might snow.

"Oh, here and there," she said. "One little town after another. But Sullivan's Falls has grown so much, what with the college and the paper mill and all, I thought I'd give this place another try."

While Margo LaRue concentrated on the eye shadow samples in front of her, I turned to Fancy and shot her a what-do-I-do-now look.

"So you've lived here before?" Fancy asked.

Margo LaRue turned and gave Fancy a curious glance, and then she said, "Yes, a long time ago."

That's when Fancy gave *me* a what-do-I-do-now look.

I shook my head and mouthed, "Nothing." I was afraid that if we tried to dig any deeper, Margo would smell a rat, pack up her bag, and hightail it. Getting anything worthwhile out of her was going to take some time.

"Well, kiddos," Margo LaRue said. "You match the shadow to your outfit. Here's a green one for you, Fancy. And you're going to have to take off your glasses, Amelia."

When I did, she pulled back and let out a tiny gasp.

"What's the matter?" I asked. Now that she could see my whole face, I figured it was making her sick and she'd have to go home.

"It's just that with your glasses on, I couldn't see how beautiful your eyes are." She kept staring at me. "And you remind me of somebody I used to know."

We are beginning to make headway is what I was thinking. "Who do I remind you of?" My insides started to quiver. This was the moment I'd been waiting for as long as I could remember.

She didn't answer, just kept examining my face. "You said your father's in the army?"

"Um—"

"He's in Rome, Italy," Fancy blurted out. "But he speaks English and everything. And Amelia looks just like him." I guess she realized that didn't make sense, since she'd just moved to Sullivan's Falls, so she added, "I've seen his picture."

Fancy's explanation must have seemed a little squirmy, because Margo LaRue looked straight at me and said, "What did you say your last name is?"

I was the one who was supposed to be asking the questions. Sometimes things just cave in on you. "Earhart," I said fast.

"Amelia Earhart," Margo LaRue said thoughtfully. "That's so beautiful. I think there used to be a movie actress with that name." I wished Grandpa Thomas could have been there for that one.

"I think you're right," I said. "Can we try on that eye stuff now?"

After Margo LaRue left, Fancy went to Shady Oaks with me to see Grandpa Thomas. She'd been there before, but that day was different. There was a new nurse's aide who thought it was her job to decide who could be there and who couldn't. Fancy was a *couldn't.*

"I'm sorry," she said when she saw us come in the door. Then she looked straight at Fancy—and not in a nice way. "Children aren't allowed in the home."

"But I always come," I said. "My grandpa, Thomas Rye, lives here."

"Well, then you're okay, but your friend will have to wait outside."

"Why?" I asked, even though I already knew what was in her head.

"Uh . . . because . . . um . . . only family members are allowed."

That was a lie. I could see she wasn't going to back down, so I had to think fast. "This is Fancy Nelson," I said, important. "She lives with Judge Watson. And she's been here before." Then I told a real whopper. "Sometimes the judge even comes with her."

That did it. "All right. Just don't stay too long," the nurse's aide said, defeated. "These old folks need their rest."

"I don't think Nurse Nasty likes little colored girls," Fancy said as we were walking down the hall.

"I don't think so either," I said on our way into Grandpa Thomas's room. "And from the sour look on her face, I'd guess she doesn't like a lot of things."

Fancy sat in the chair by the window and read the new issue of the *American Girl* magazine she'd found in her mailbox when we left her house.

Grandpa Thomas was taking a nap, and snoring like his regular old self. It was easier when he was asleep. I could pretend that he hadn't gone off to that strange, silent world where he lived when he was awake. I sat in the chair next to his bed and whispered so I wouldn't disturb him. "I met her," I said.

Who?

"Daddy's girlfriend."

Oh, her. Does she still look like a joke?

"Yeah. She's pretty funny-looking."

So, where's your father been hiding all these years?

"I have no idea."

She wouldn't tell you? That's a hell of a thing. It's the least she could do.

"I didn't ask her."

Why not?

"I don't know. I'll try to find out more if I see her again. Besides, she's real nice to me and I don't want to scare her away."

Well, from what I've heard, she's been real nice to a lot of people.

I didn't say anything more to Grandpa Thomas, just sat there and watched him sleep. I couldn't even tell *him* what I was thinking—that I understood what Daddy saw in Margo LaRue and I wished I could move in with her, too—so *she* could be my mother.

7

Raspberries and Wonder bread

Your sister Sylvia's taking some time off from the slipper factory and she's coming for a visit," Mama said as I was handing her a glass of iced tea. It was mid-August and the heat was so bad, the moisture from the outside of the glass ran down my arm and dripped onto her skirt. I expected her to snap at me, but when she didn't, I sat next to her on the porch swing. She was holding a letter that had come in the mail that morning, one I had steamed open and then glued back shut.

"When'll she get here?" I asked, even though I already knew the answer. I was so excited. Nobody ever came to visit. Maybe Sylvia might even decide to stay. Now that Sullivan's Falls was getting bigger, there were Help Wanted signs all over the place. My nephew, William, could have my room. I wouldn't mind sleeping on the couch if it meant having a real family. Sylvia wrote that she had something important to discuss with Mama. Maybe moving to Sullivan's Falls was it.

"They're coming on Saturday," Mama answered, wiping her forehead with the handkerchief she kept tucked down her front. She was wearing a sleeveless blouse, and the wrinkled skin under her arm whipped back and forth like a flag in the wind. "She finally talked that poor excuse for a husband of hers into getting her on down here."

I'd heard how useless Sam was for as long as I could remember. And how nobody in their right mind, let alone her very own daughter, would marry a man with only one leg. It didn't even matter that Sylvia claimed he'd lost it when he was blown up in Pearl Harbor, defending his country. People with missing pieces gave Mama the shivers.

"Are they going to stay for a while?" I asked. Sylvia didn't mention how long they'd be visiting, but I figured I'd better act curious or Mama might connect the hole on the back of the envelope to me. How could I know that rubbing glue off paper with a wet dishrag was not a good idea—especially since I'd been warned my whole life not to open the mail?

"I'm not sure how long they'll stay," Mama said.

She started rocking the swing just the slightest bit, got all dreamy-eyed, and changed to a different subject. "When Charlotte was little," she said, tender, "we used to sit out here for hours. She'd snuggle in close and I'd hold her hand and we'd watch the world go by. She was a real mama's girl."

Mama was in such a good mood, and the world was still going by, so I scooched over and laid my hand on her lap in case she decided she wanted to hold it. She didn't. She just ignored it and sipped her iced tea, so I took my hand back and pretended that my nose needed scratching. I could taste the salt of a runaway tear on my lip, and the heat from my embarrassment rose from the depths of me, up my neck to my face. But Mama didn't notice. Looking at me was not something she did very often.

"What about Jack?" I said when the fire had left my face. "Was he a mama's boy?" This was the first time I'd ever asked her anything about my brother. Sometimes you just stay away from a topic, especially when you know it's a person's sore spot. But right then I wanted to put my thumb on that spot and push until it hurt. Mama deserved it for making me feel worthless.

She looked at me as if I'd asked if we were having boiled rat for supper. "Mama's boy! Of course not! What are you talking about?"

I was talking about the fact that Jack had run away from home when he was in high school because she made such a big deal about him being a preacher's kid, saying that he should always behave like a gentleman and set a good example for the other boys in town. Grandpa Thomas said that she made Jack wear a suit and tie to school and wouldn't let him get dirty, even when he was little. The kids taunted him so bad, he finally couldn't take it anymore and left, hitchhiked all the way to New York City. Nobody knew where he'd gone until he was eighteen and his picture appeared in the paper. In place of a suit, he was wearing a striped uniform, and handcuffs instead of a tie. After that, Mama'd given him up for dead and never mentioned his name again.

"I was just wondering what he was like," I said.

"Well, you can stop wondering about things that don't concern you." She fanned her face with Sylvia's letter and gave me a shove with her hip. "I need some room," she said, impatient. "It's too hot to have you hanging all over me."

I hated her so much, and that is not how a girl is supposed to feel toward her own mother. Anybody will tell you that. When I have my own little girl and it is a hot, muggy day, I will sit with her on our front porch and I will hug her and hold her hand and bury my face in her hair and tell her that she is pretty, even if she isn't, and that she smells like a sweet, juicy peach, ripe for the picking, and we'll admire the blood-red geraniums we planted together—like the ones Fancy and her mother planted along their sidewalk and in the huge cement containers on the front lawn next to their flagpole. And I will never even tell her that she had a grandmother.

On Saturday, I was sitting on the front porch steps, staying out of Mama's range of fire, when a green and white '53 Chevy Bel Air convertible with the top down pulled up in front of the house. I could hear William before I saw him slouched in the backseat. "I told you. I'm not getting out of the car. I don't know that old woman. And who's that four-eyes on the porch? She's staring at me!" The joy I felt about meeting him and all the plans I'd made about the things we'd do while he was visiting were washed away by his whiny voice and hateful words.

Sylvia chimed in. "Nobody's staring at you! That's just your aunt Amelia." Then she lowered her voice. "Now try to be civil. We're not going to be here long— just until we get what we came for."

That's what happens when you get your hopes up too high. They usually collapse. I have found that it is best to think the worst so you will be prepared. And if things do turn out right, well then good. Sylvia wasn't going to settle down in Sullivan's Falls with us. Plus, I should have known that William would be a jerk. Other than Grandpa Thomas, it was becoming clear that my whole family could have been the main attraction in a freak show.

When Sylvia opened the car door, William hollered, "You can't make me go in there, so don't even try!"

Sylvia's tone went limp. "Just come in for a few minutes to be polite."

William stood up, glared at Sylvia, and said, "You might as well drop it because I'm not going anywhere." Then he blew his mother a raspberry—a big, loud, juicy raspberry. If I ever did that to Mama, I'd be ice-cold dead. In fact, after she murdered me, she'd kill me again to make sure I'd learned my lesson.

But Sylvia didn't bawl him out or anything, she only said, "Now, William, don't work yourself into a fit. You'll get a stomachache." She stroked his cheek. "And I didn't mean to upset you. Just come in when you're ready. Okay?"

Wow! If that wasn't a fit, what was? I sure hoped he'd work himself into one. I'd've loved to see that.

When Sam got out of the car and walked over to Sylvia, he didn't limp or anything. I'm ashamed to say this, but while they were walking toward me, I was trying to figure out which leg was fake. And it made me feel wicked, as if I was like Mama, more interested in that one thing than I was in the rest of him, which was not what I expected. I thought he'd be all army neat. Instead, he looked a lot like one of those guys in a gangster movie with slicked-down hair and a toothpick in his mouth for show.

Sylvia was built round and soft like Mama, with the same pug nose and frizzed-up hair you get if you leave the Toni home permanent rollers on too long. "Hello, Amelia," she said, pleasant. "I'm sorry we didn't come sooner. But until now, we just couldn't find the time to make such a long trip." Then she glanced over at the Chevy. "And William's finally gotten over his car sickness problem." She touched my shoulder. "Well, anyway, I'm glad to finally meet you."

"Me, too," I said. I stood up, and she hugged me, genuine. I hugged her back. Maybe this wasn't going to be so bad after all.

We both ran out of words, so we just stood there, smiling at each other. Finally she said, "What grade are you in?"

"Going into fifth," I answered. "I'm ten."

"Fifth?" she said, way too enthused. "That's wonderful! And *ten* already. Imagine that!"

"Yup."

More smiling.

"Oh, and this is my husband, Sam," Sylvia said. There was not what you would call love in her voice when she mentioned his name.

"Hey, kid. How ya doing?" Sam said, in a regular voice—not gangster.

"Fine," I answered.

"So what's Ma up to?" Sylvia asked, in kind of a mean tone. This surprised me because I thought she'd be excited to see Mama after so many years.

"She's in the kitchen, making potato salad. She said it's your favorite."

Sylvia laughed a little in her throat. "Since when has she ever done anything special for me? It's her precious Charlotte who loves potato salad. I can't stand that stuff." Then she said, "Come on, Sam, I guess we'd better go in."

As I was moving over to let them by, Sam patted my head, then pointed toward the car. "See if you can convince Willie to come join the party. He's in a snit, though, so keep your distance." He winked at me, and followed Sylvia in the front door.

William was deep into a comic book and didn't hear me coming. I said, "Hi, Willie! I'm Amelia."

You should have seen him jump—at least a foot off that dark green vinyl seat, which must have been a million and a half degrees hot.

"You sure are nervous, Willie. Sorry I scared you," I said, although I was not one bit sorry. He had it coming for calling me *four-eyes*.

He glared at me and said, "What do you want?"

"Aren't you coming in the house?"

"Who wants to know?" I was beginning to think

that William was a little low in the brains department.

"I just figured you might be hot."

"Well, I'm not. Besides, we're only going to be here long enough to get your mother to sign the will."

I looked at William, hard. "What will?"

"The one that leaves this house to my mother when your mother dies."

The fear that crept into my head surprised me. Hating Mama was one thing, but thinking about her being dead was not something I wanted to do. "My mother's not going to die," I said. "She's not even sick."

"That's not what I heard," he answered, in a know-it-all way.

Something strong started squeezing my chest. "What did you hear?"

"That she's got a bad ticker and could keel over any minute."

I knew Mama'd gone to the doctor, but she didn't mention anything about her heart being on the fritz. "I think you're making this up just to be rotten," I said, hoping he didn't notice the panic in my voice.

"Think what you want. But when you're an orphan with no place to live, you'll believe it all right. After we sell your mom's house, we'll be on easy street."

Something deep inside my brain that had been sleeping for a long time woke up, and I had to fight the urge to start counting. Then I remembered Daddy. "I wouldn't be an orphan," I said. "I have a father. He'd come and live in our house and take care of me." Of course. That's what would happen. If Mama wasn't there to stir up trouble, Daddy would come home in a second. All of a sudden I could breathe again.

"Your father?" William said, with an evil glint in his eye. "You must mean my grandpa Rye. He came to visit us a few years ago. He's real nice." William pointed at the house. "Ma said he left this stupid town because your mama drove him away."

The fact that this miserable weasel had met my daddy—and I hadn't—made my blood boil. But I reined myself in and said, sweet, "I'm glad you got to meet him." And then I changed my voice to slow casual, like I was talking about the weather and didn't really care one way or the other. "What's he like anyway? I mean other than being nice."

"He's tall."

Oh, brother. "What else?"

"What else *what*?"

"Besides being tall, what's he like?"

"I think he has brown hair."

Well, for crying out loud! "I don't mean what he looks like. I mean what's he *like*?"

"I told you. He's nice." William picked up his Spider-Man comic and started reading.

"Did he say anything about me?" That one slipped

out before I could catch it. I was pretty sure William was playing me like I was a fish nibbling on a line, and I didn't want to get caught.

He looked over at me, annoyed, like Spider-Man would get mad and crawl away if William ignored him. He put down the comic, stared straight at me, and said, "I can't remember anything else."

I bet my daddy did mention me, and William was too much of a snot to say so. I took a deep breath. Here was my chance. "Well, do you know *where* he is?"

"Maybe." William smiled. "But I don't think he'd come all the way back here just to take care of a kid he's never even met."

I stood my ground. If I kept at him, maybe he would crack. "All the way back from where?" I said, as cool as ice.

But William was less of a fool than I thought. He waggled his head back and forth in a nyah, nyah kind of way as he said, "That's for me to know and for you to find out." And you would not believe the smirky look that rat gave me because he knew he had me good.

I didn't know what else to say, so I just stood there, staring at William's pale brown eyes. Then, out of the blue, I saw Fancy. She was riding toward us on her bike—no hands—carrying a loaf of bread.

"Who's that?" William said, pointing down the sidewalk.

Before I had a chance to answer, Fancy said, "Hi, Amelia." She put on the brakes, grabbed the car door to balance herself, and held up the bread. "My mother sent me to the store. What's going on?"

Having Fancy there made things feel a little bit normal. "Nothing much," I answered. "Just shooting the breeze with my nephew, Willie. Remember? I told you he was coming."

"Oh, right," Fancy said to William. "You're the one who lives up in Maine. Nice to meet you. I'm Amelia's friend, Fancy."

William pulled back. "You don't look fancy to me. You look like a dirty little colored girl. And get your hand off my car."

A gasp escaped my mouth. And before I knew what was happening, I'd grabbed the loaf of bread from Fancy and smacked William with it.

William rubbed his shoulder and yelled, *"Ouch!"* as if I'd clobbered him with a brick.

Fancy reached for the bread. "Give me that," she hollered. "My mother's making egg salad sandwiches for lunch. Now they're going to be all smashed. Thanks a lot!"

"But he said you were dirty. He shouldn't have done that."

"He's just stupid, that's all. And he sure isn't worth ruining a perfectly good loaf of bread."

"At least my skin looks clean," William said to Fancy.

Fancy rolled her eyes as if she couldn't believe how hopeless William was. Then she took the bread and started to pedal. As she was riding away, she yelled back, "As soon as he leaves, come over to my house. I have something to show you. Oh, and Willie. You need to work on your insults. I've been called a lot worse than *dirty*."

I looked over at the house, and Sam was standing on the porch, smoking. When he started walking toward me, I expected him to chew me out for smacking his precious Willie. But when he reached the car, he put his hand on my shoulder. "That's quite an arm you got there. Too bad it was only a loaf of bread. I wish you'd have knocked the snot out of that little milquetoast mama's boy."

William didn't say a word. Just hung his head and sat there.

On his way back to the house, Sam took a long drag on his cigarette, dropped it on the sidewalk, and pulverized it with his shoe. Then he called, "Oh, by the way, Amelia, your ma sent me out here to tell you that lunch is ready."

The mean way Sam talked about his own son right in front of him made me feel sick, the way I felt when Mama looked at me like she wished I was dead.

I touched William's arm, gentle. "Come on," I said. "Let's go have something to eat."

He swatted my hand away and yelled, "Leave me alone!"

As I was walking toward the house, I thought maybe it wasn't Mama and me that William wanted to stay away from. Maybe it was his own daddy.

8

Cheeseburgers, root beer floats, and chocolate-covered dentures

I t's too crowded back here," William said. "I want to sit by the door." We were in the car on our way to visit Grandpa Thomas—even Mama—which was just a show for Sylvia, because Mama'd never been to see him, not once. "And I'm hungry," William added. "There's an A&W right over there. I want two cheeseburgers, French fries, and a root beer float with extra ice cream."

Up until then, Mama'd stayed quiet. Even when William wouldn't shake her hand while everybody was getting in the car and she was making a big fuss and lying about how nice-looking he was and how she wished she'd met him sooner. Even when William pointed out that Mama's mustache was the best one he'd ever seen on a woman. "We just *had* hamburgers," she said, her eyes blazing. "And fried chicken and potato salad and baked beans and deviled eggs and watermelon and peach pie and ice cream and homemade lemonade. Your father said you weren't hungry."

"I *wasn't* hungry then," William replied. "But now I am."

I stopped breathing and braced myself to witness the murder.

Mama took a deep breath, puffed out her cheeks, and her face turned so red, I thought she was going to blow up. She reached across me and wagged her finger in William's face. "Now look here—"

"Ma!" Sylvia cut in. "You keep out of this. He's *my* kid and he can have a hamburger if he wants one."

"What's the matter with you—letting him act like a fool," Mama said, shooting William one of her famous evil eyes.

Willie ignored the insult and told Sam to pull into the A&W parking lot. "There's a good spot right next to that blue Nash."

"Sure, son," Sam said.

It made me want to gag—the way Sam kowtowed to William when Sylvia was there and then made him feel like two cents when she wasn't around to hear.

Sam gave Mama a quick peek over his shoulder. "It'll only take a minute, Mother Rye. The boy needs his nourishment."

That made Mama aim her venom at Sam. "Don't

you *ever* call me Mother." She leaned forward in her seat till her mouth was right next to Sam's ear. "And don't you think for one minute that your phony act is fooling me. You're nothing but a lazy, good-for-nothing bum who's made a fool of my daughter, and now you've convinced her to pick the meat off my carcass." To make sure she had his full attention, she jabbed him in the shoulder with her finger. "You sit at home and do nothing while Sylvia works all those hours to support you and that kid of yours. You ought to be ashamed of yourself." When she ran out of steam, she sat back and crossed her arms so tight, her knuckles turned as white as Sylvia's lipstick.

Then Sylvia started in again. "Ma, you have no right to talk to Sam like that. He drove us all the way here to make sure things are in order in case anything bad happens to you, so you won't have to worry and make yourself even sicker." Then things got really scary. "Besides, he was nice enough to agree to take Amelia in if a tragedy happens. You should be thanking him instead of giving him grief."

You can bet my stomach fell straight to the ground when I heard her say that. I would rather have lived in a ditch than with this bunch of crazies. I was beginning to realize that a family is a lot more than just having all the rooms in your house filled up.

"Thanking him?" Mama said, her voice rising an octave. "I should be thanking him for stealing my house because it's the only way he'll agree to give your little sister a place to live when I'm gone?" Mama stopped for a second. "Come to think of it, that part isn't even on the paper I signed. How do I know you really *will* take her in? And what about poor Charlotte? Some of that money should go to her."

Sylvia looked back at Mama like she'd love to kill her and said, "We'll take Amelia in because we promised we would, but what's Charlotte going to do with money? She doesn't even know who she is. And there's no way in hell we could support another kid without the money from that house."

Mama's eyes went wild. "I didn't raise you to use bad language."

"You didn't raise me, Ma. You put up with me." Sylvia's voice was low and slow and she gave each word special attention. "You treated me like a weed while your beautiful Charlotte got the spotlight. And now look where she is." She glanced back at me. "In fact, look at all of us. No wonder Daddy took off! And why do you think I haven't been back? I couldn't wait to get away from you. And as far as the house—you owe me at least that much."

I expected Mama to have a conniption. But she didn't do anything, just sat there like she'd been shot but hadn't fallen over yet. Then Sylvia turned around and everybody clammed up and waited for William to give the carhop his order.

"I'll sit over by that tree," William said when we got to the nursing home. "I don't know that man in there and I want to finish my comic book." Nobody objected. I think even Sylvia needed a break from William.

"I'll stay in the car," Mama said. "I was just here the other day." The fact that she could lie bald-faced like that scared me. You would think somebody as God-fearing as she was would watch her step, especially if it was true that she could drop dead any second. Maybe, along with my bad eyes, I'd gotten my talent for lying from her.

"I'll wait with you," I said. All that talk about tragedies and wills and stuff—and especially me living with Sam and Sylvia and William—made me want to stay close to Mama. Sometimes you find out that you are not as bad off as you thought you were. And maybe if Mama hadn't been all worn out when I was born, she could have loved me just a little bit.

"We won't be long," Sam said nice, as if the bad talk had never happened. "We have to head back to Maine as soon as we're finished here. Sylvia has to work tomorrow."

After they were gone, Mama leaned her head against the back of the seat and I waited till I worked up the courage to say, "I don't want you to die."

She opened her eyes and looked over at me, not

mean or anything. "A lot of people have bad hearts and they live forever. I probably will, too."

"I hope so, but Sylvia made it sound like it could happen any day."

Mama closed her eyes again, took in a big breath, and sighed. "I guess that's what she's hoping for." A tear ran down her cheek, and when I reached over to wipe it off, she took hold of my hand. She didn't slap it, just held it for the first time ever. "I only wish I knew where your father was."

"Me, too," I said.

"Now, I just need to take a little nap," Mama said, low. "Why don't you go in and say hello to your grandfather? After they leave, I'll make you a grilled cheese sandwich for supper—with bacon, just the way you like it." She gave my hand a tiny squeeze before she let go. "And don't worry about me dying. I made it sound a lot worse than it really is because I wanted Sylvia to come home." She shook her head. "I got a lot more than I bargained for."

As I walked away, I wondered if things between Mama and me might be going to change. Up until then, she'd had Sylvia. But now, I was all she had left. Maybe that would be enough.

Grandpa Thomas was sitting on the red plastic chair in the corner of his room, and Sam was standing by the window, smoking a cigarette. Sylvia was

feeding Grandpa Thomas a dish of chocolate pudding.

"Let *go!*" Sylvia said, trying to pry Grandpa
Thomas's jaw open so she could get the spoon out of
his mouth. "I can't give you any more if you don't let
go." Her voice was strict, like she was talking to a
naughty child. I would have jumped in, but I knew
what was coming next was way better than any
tongue-lashing I could have given her. I'd seen it happen when Nurse Nasty was giving Grandpa Thomas a
hard time with a bowl of smashed-up spaghetti, so I
just stood back and waited.

"Open your mouth *now!*" Sylvia said, yanking on
the spoon with both hands.

When Grandpa Thomas did, I heard *schloop!* Then
his false teeth flew out, skittering down the front of
Sylvia's white skirt, and she bolted from the room as if
she was trying to outrun a tornado.

Other than being a little caved in, Grandpa
Thomas's face looked like it always did—plain. But I
would swear on a truckload of Bibles that he had the
tiniest bit of a twinkle in his eye. I had always suspected that there was more going on inside his head
than he could let on to the outside world.

Sam squashed the tip of his cigarette on the sole of
his shoe, then parked it behind his left ear for later.
He walked over to the red chair. "We have to be going,
but it was sure nice to see you, sir," he said, shaking

Grandpa Thomas's hand real slow and for way too long. That's when I realized there was more than just shaking going on. Like a sleight-of-hand magician, Sam slid Grandpa Thomas's watch over his thin wrist and palmed it. Then he dropped it in his own pocket and started for the door.

I planted myself in front of him, clenched my teeth, and said, "Give me that!"

But he just shoved me aside. "You'd better keep your big mouth shut."

I jumped ahead of him again and reached into his pocket. "That's Grandpa Thomas's watch. It's real gold—fourteen karat. He won it in a poker game fair and square. Give it back!"

Sam squeezed my hand so hard I let out a squeal, and the watch dropped back to the bottom of his pocket. "It's not doing him any good," he said. "And he shouldn't have been gambling anyway. Besides, mine's broke and I need one to get to work on time."

"You don't even have a job!"

"Well, I might get myself one, and if I do, I'll need a watch."

"I'm going to tell my mother you stole Grandpa Thomas's watch and she'll make you give it back. And I bet as soon as you leave, she'll change her will."

"She won't change her will because she knows that there's nobody else who'll take you."

"I'm going to tell her anyway."

"You do and I'll tell her how chummy you are with that colored girl. I bet she doesn't know you have a little darkie friend. I noticed you didn't invite her in. And where'd a kid like that get a top-of-the-line Schwinn? She has to have swiped it. Did you ever think of that?"

The stupid jerk had me. He could have stolen the eyeballs right out of my head and I'd have kept quiet about it if it meant losing Fancy.

"Take the watch," I said, moving out of his way. "I won't say anything."

He patted my cheek, which made me cringe. "Now you're talking," he said, all satisfied. "Let's go. I have to drop you and your ma off and get out of this one-horse town."

"I'll walk home," I answered, smart-assy. "And if you think I'm ever going to go live with you, you're nuts."

"That's fine with me," he said. "When your ma dies, you can move down to the slums with those sticky-fingered Negroes you're so fond of." Then he left—didn't say bye or anything. As he walked away, I still could not tell which leg was wood. I bet that whole story about him being a war hero was just a big fat lie. No war hero would ever steal a helpless old man's watch.

After Sam was gone, I took Grandpa Thomas's teeth to the bathroom and gave them a good scrub. When they were back where they belonged, I fed him the pudding, but I didn't mention how Sylvia'd swindled the house out of Mama. Maybe Sylvia was right. Mama probably did owe her at least that much. Plus, Fancy's house was big, and I was pretty sure Mrs. Nelson liked me. Maybe, if Mama did die, I really could go live with them.

9

Secrets, lies, and chicken noodle soup

After I left Shady Oaks and started home, I remembered that Fancy wanted to show me something. When I stopped at her house, she was sitting at the white wicker table on the front porch, working on a paint-by-number picture of dalmatians playing baseball. She jumped up, grabbed my hand, and headed for the door. "Come upstairs," she said in a whisper. "And don't make any noise."

"Why not?" I asked. I figured Judge Watson was taking a nap or maybe her mother had a headache. We always made as much noise as we wanted to and nobody'd ever complained about it.

"My mother's around here somewhere and I don't want her to know what we're doing."

This surprised me because Fancy shared things with her mother all the time that I never would have told Mama. Like when she got in trouble at school and how she couldn't wait to kiss a boy and that her ninnies might be starting to grow—personal junk like that. "What are we going to be doing?" I asked. I hoped she didn't want to play taxi again—that's a game where we made sure the yellow Studebaker was gone, then called a cab and watched out the window while the driver waited for Margo LaRue, who, of course, never came out of the house. Then we'd giggle as he finally drove away in a huff. You can be sure that my heart was beating fast while I wondered if kids could be arrested for pulling a stunt like that.

Instead of going down the hall to Fancy's room, we stopped in front of Judge Watson's door. I thought she just wanted to tell me something. But no. She turned the knob and pulled me inside. It smelled like leather and cigars and man soap and furniture polish and new-cut grass. I remember thinking, now *this* is what an old house is supposed to be like—everything dark and heavy and mysterious—even one of those four-poster beds with a carved wooden top, thick, tied-back curtains surrounding it like a theater stage, and a mattress so high you had to walk up little steps to climb in.

Fancy headed straight for the desk by the open window and I grabbed her shirt and followed like we were Siamese twins. As exciting as it was to be in such a spooky place, the fact that it belonged to Judge

Watson was another matter entirely. I felt as if I might be breaking a law just being there. I didn't expect him to jump out of a closet and kill me or anything like that. It's just that he was different from everybody else in Sullivan's Falls—better. Not even because he wanted to be. He just was. And ordinary people had no business poking around his things.

The first time I stayed for supper at Fancy's, it surprised me that he even ate. It was like watching God eat. He sat at the head of the table and carved the roast beef with a fancy silver knife-and-fork set, the kind the queen of England might use if she decided to cut her own meat. After we were all served, he asked us to bow our heads and he said grace, low and slow and important-sounding. And you just knew that the real God had stopped whatever He was doing and was listening with His own head bowed.

"There's your mother," I said, looking out the window. "She's in the back yard—doing *something*." The gardener was mowing the lawn, but Mrs. Nelson was on her hands and knees under a lilac tree. She was wearing dungarees and tennis shoes, which, as far as I knew, mothers were not allowed to do.

Fancy stopped rummaging around in the top drawer of the desk and glanced out the window. "Oh, good. She's working on her rock garden. She'll be out there for hours. We can take our time."

It amazed me that perfect Mrs. Nelson liked to

crawl around in the dirt. "But what about the judge?" I worried. "When's he coming home?"

"Not till dinnertime," she answered, holding up an old-fashioned key on a ring that looked like real gold. "This is his day to play golf."

That was not something I'd ever pictured—Judge Watson in one of those V-neck sweater outfits, chasing after a little white ball. I'd never seen him in anything but a black suit, acting formal.

By then, Fancy'd unlocked the bottom drawer of the desk, hauled out a banged-up metal box, and scattered its contents on the rug.

"What's all that?" I asked, wondering what could be so interesting about a bunch of ancient-looking papers.

"Just wait a sec. You'll see." Her butt was flat on the floor and her legs were splayed out funny behind her—just one of the creepy things she can do because she's double-jointed. When she settled in like that, I knew we'd be there for a while.

"Why don't we go do something fun?" I groaned. "That stuff smells like wet moss and it looks a thousand years old." Fancy's favorite subject was history, so I figured she'd discovered another boring fact about Abraham Lincoln or one of the other famous dead people she was always talking about. "Let's go play taxi," I said out of desperation.

She ignored me and started sorting through papers. When she came to an envelope that was so frayed the edges were falling apart, she hugged it to her chest and looked straight into my eyes. "You have to promise that you'll never tell a soul about this."

That's when things got interesting. If a promise is involved, there's usually juice to go along with it. "Who would I tell?" I said, in a smart-ass voice. "You're the only friend I have, and even you won't be able to pry it out of me." I thought that last part was funny. She didn't.

"I *mean* it," she said all mad-sounding. "You can't tell *anybody*."

"I won't!" My feelings were hurt because I thought she had more confidence in me than that, but I could tell by her face that this was important to her, so I behaved myself and made my voice sound somber. "I promise. I won't say a thing to anybody."

"Okay then." She took a deep breath—the kind that comes back out all quivery—opened the envelope, and handed me a paper. "Read this," she said, as if I was about to find out that the world was coming to an end. "Just be careful with it."

I didn't snap at her like I wanted to and say that I could see it was fragile and needed to be treated gently, because she was sitting there with her folded hands pressed over her mouth and anticipation in her eyes that was so fierce it could have been a live thing. You have to give a person a little extra when they are wound that tight.

"What does *this* have to do with anything?" I asked after I'd looked at it.

"It's a birth certificate."

"Well, I can *see* that. But whose is it?" I didn't know anybody named Genevieve Marguerite Watson who was born in Hartsville, Alabama, in 1929. And Fancy'd never mentioned her.

Fancy pointed to the bottom of the page. "Look at the father's name."

"Martin Earl Watson," I read out loud. "That's probably the judge."

"It is."

"Yeah, so? He was married and had a kid. What's the big deal about that?"

"Look at the mother's name."

"Sarah Marguerite Bowen," I said, and then thought for a minute. "That can't be his wife. She has a different last name. Who's she?"

"My granny."

Sometimes a tedious subject picks up speed and gets your attention fast. "Well, then that means . . ."

"The judge is my grandfather," Fancy whispered.

This was *big*. "But who's Genevieve Marguerite Watson?"

She looked at me as if I should have already figured that one out. "My *mother*."

"But your mother's last name is Nelson."

Fancy rolled her eyes. "She got married!" She didn't add the *dummy* part, but I knew that's what she was thinking.

"Oh. That's right. I forgot." I'm what you would call medium smart, but Fancy's a genius, so she doesn't always have a lot of patience with me. She just sat there, and I figured she was waiting for me to say something else, so I added, "Does your mother know you know?"

"Of course not. I'd have to tell her I'd been snooping through the judge's desk and I'd be grounded forever. I'm not even supposed to come in here." Her voice changed to angry. "Besides, she should have told me. It's my business as much as it is hers."

I wondered why she hadn't. As far as I was concerned, anybody'd be proud to have Judge Watson for a relative. But Fancy and I weren't old enough to know that if your mama and daddy aren't married it's not something you brag about. And the fact that Judge Watson had a baby with his colored maid muddied up the secret even more.

"Maybe she's just waiting till you're older." I didn't know what I was talking about, but I thought I should say something.

"Yeah, probably." She put the paper back in the envelope. "It doesn't matter anyway," she added. "If I could choose a grandfather, he'd be the one." But then her face clouded over.

"What's the matter?" I asked.

She stared at her hands. "He never takes us anywhere. Maybe he's ashamed of me. And my mother, too."

I knew what she was thinking, and I hoped it wasn't true. "He probably just doesn't like to go places."

She shrugged. "I don't know. Could be."

The lawn mower backfired, and I looked down into the yard. "Your mother's not in her rock garden," I said, kind of in a panic. "I don't see her anywhere."

"Quick! Help me put this back!" Fancy said. "When she doesn't find me on the porch, she's gonna come looking."

I started stuffing papers into the metal box, and she dumped them right back out. "They have to go in a certain way. The judge is really particular about keeping things in order."

I already knew that because of the way the rest of the room looked and how the top of his desk was arranged with everything perfect, even the pens lined up in a straight row. "Well, hurry up then," I said. "I think I just heard the front door open."

"I'm never going to get this stuff back in time. You

go down and stall her. Just make up something and tell her I'll be right there."

"You want me to lie to your mother?"

"*Yes*, I want you to lie to my mother. I want you to tackle her and hold her down if you have to. She *can't* find me here."

"But what should I say?"

"I don't care what you say. Just keep her down there. Now go!"

"Okay, but hurry up." The thought of talking to Mrs. Nelson without Fancy there balled my stomach up good.

"Hi, Mrs. Nelson," I said when I got to the bottom of the stairs. She'd just come in the front door and was headed my way. Even in her work clothes, she looked classy, like one of those runway models you see in *Vogue* magazine.

"Oh, hi, Amelia," she said, out of breath. "I'm looking for Fancy. Is she upstairs?"

"Yes. She's in the bathroom. I just walked her up. She's not doing anything else up there—just going to the bathroom. She was working on her painting until a minute ago. I decided to go with her so she wouldn't be lonely. I know *I* hate to go to the bathroom alone." Well, for Pete's sake. If Sullivan's Falls ever decided to have a stupid contest, I'd win—hands down.

Maybe Mrs. Nelson thought I was a little on the slow side, because she didn't let on that what I'd just said sounded as if it had come from a moron. "Well then, why don't we wait for her on the porch?" she said. "It's a beautiful day."

"That's a good idea. I love porches." I wanted to kill Fancy. Having a conversation with an adult was so hard for me, while she could have gabbed for hours with President Kennedy himself and enjoyed it.

Mrs. Nelson led me out the door and over to a white metal glider with puffy yellow cushions. She motioned for me to sit down, then sat next to me close and patted my knee. When she smiled, her eyes reminded me of Judge Watson. If you didn't count his white hair, his deep blue eyes were what you noticed first. "So," she said. "Fancy told me you had family visiting from Maine."

Oh, man. I hoped Fancy hadn't given the details about why her bread was in such bad shape and that William was the biggest creep she'd ever met. "I did," I said. "But they're gone now."

She made a clucking noise with her tongue. "It's too bad they couldn't stay longer." She brushed a piece of dirt off her blouse sleeve. "And how's your mother doing? I hope she's not wearing herself out in her garden. Fancy says her flowers are beautiful."

Beautiful? Our entire yard was one gigantic weed. A flower wouldn't even know how to act there. "No. She's fine," I said. "She loves working outside." I was beginning to realize that *I* was Fancy's Faith Divine.

Mrs. Nelson pointed to the grass stains on her dungarees. "As you can see, I do, too. Maybe your mother and I can get together someday. I'm sure she's just as sweet as you are."

"My mother *is* sweet," I answered. "But she doesn't really like to do things with other people. She just keeps busy at home." I hated lying to Mrs. Nelson, so when Fancy came out and sat next to her mother, I got her back. "I hope you're feeling better," I said in a worried voice.

"What are you talking about?" Fancy asked.

"You told me how sick you felt."

"I didn't know you were sick, sweetie," Mrs. Nelson said, concerned.

"I'm not sick," Fancy said, annoyed. "Where'd you get that idea?"

"Sure you are," I added. "You told me you had a terrible stomachache. That's why you were in the bathroom so long, right?"

Fancy glared at me. "Right," she said, straight-line angry.

Mrs. Nelson put her hand on Fancy's forehead. "You are warm, honey. I'm going to tuck you in bed, and a little later, I'll bring you a nice bowl of chicken noodle soup for dinner."

I thought about the times I'd been sick and had to make my own soup. Sometimes being around Fancy and her mother just made me feel pure awful.

Fancy didn't say anything about the fact that she felt a little warm because it was ninety degrees out and how much she was looking forward to the spaghetti and meatballs her mother was making for dinner.

I smiled at her, as sweet as a maple sugar pie, and said, "Well, I'd better leave now and let you go to bed. Plus, I don't want to miss the special dinner my mother's making. After she finishes working in her flower garden, that is. See you later, Fancy. And it was nice talking to you, Mrs. Nelson."

"You, too, Amelia," Mrs. Nelson said. "Come back soon."

When I got home, Mama kept her word about my grilled cheese and bacon sandwich—even included potato chips and an extra-sour dill pickle on the side. But after that, things slid right back to where they were before Sylvia came. I should have known that one tender moment does not always change a person and that I was still going to have to walk with an easy step when I was around my mother.

Was my daddy *ever* going to come and rescue me?

10

Red roses don't always mean love.

Are you sure it was *my* mother?" I asked Fancy in disbelief. "*My* mother came *here*? This *morning*?" It was the Saturday after Sylvia's visit, and Fancy and I were in her room playing Monopoly. Mama had left for work at eight o'clock that day. She said the A&P was having an early-bird special on beef and she had to be there for the rush.

"I'm positive," Fancy said as she rolled the dice. "She had an appointment to see the judge about something. I was in my pajamas, watching cartoons in the living room, when my mother answered the door. I heard them talking."

"But how do you know it was her?" As far as I knew, Fancy didn't even know what my mother looked like.

"Yay! I landed on Park Place," Fancy gloated. "Now

I've got 'em both." She waggled her finger in front of my nose and grinned huge. "You're a dead duck, Rye."

"Okay. Okay. I give up," I said, impatient. "Now how do you know it was my mother?"

"Ha! You gave up, so I won again," Fancy said. She did a little victory dance around the Monopoly board.

"Fancy!" I hollered. I was ready to smack her.

"What?"

"How do you know?"

"How do I know what?"

Sometimes she is such a pain. Maybe really smart people think about a bunch of things at the same time and the dull stuff gets pushed to the back. I grabbed her hand, pulled her down next to me, and looked straight at her. "How do you know the woman was my mother?"

"Because she *said* so. Do you want to play one more game?" I guess when you have a normal mother that you don't try to hide, the whole subject is just one big yawn.

"What do you mean she said so? What did she say—exactly?"

"She told my mother she was Allie Rye. And my mother asked if you were her daughter."

It always surprised me that my mother had a first name, and a sweet one like Allie was certainly not right for her—Mildred, maybe, or Mabel, something with hard sounds in it. "*And . . . ?*"

Fancy looked at me as if I'd grown a beard. "She said *yes*."

"What else did she say?"

"I don't know," Fancy said, exasperated. "I can't remember. Just that she had an appointment to see the judge. What's the big deal?"

It *was* a huge deal. Mama didn't go around making appointments with anybody—especially judges. I had no idea why she'd want to talk to him. But I knew that, whatever the reason, it wasn't good.

"She did say something that was kind of funny," Fancy added.

"Funny?" That was the first time anyone ever said my mother was funny.

"Not ha-ha funny. Strange funny."

Well, *that* I could believe. "What'd she say?"

"After she found out that we're friends, she asked me if Fancy is a nickname for Faith. I can't imagine where she got *that* idea."

My face turned hot. "I can't either," I said too fast and too loud. "She probably just got mixed up because they both start with *F*."

Fancy had her hands clasped together in her lap. She shrugged her shoulders and spread out her thumbs to form a wide *V*. "Yeah, probably. At least now she knows I'm not some kid named Faith."

Mama was going to kill me for lying to her. "What did she talk to the judge about?" Maybe she came to have him set me up with one of those foster families you hear about—in case something bad *did* happen to her. Sam probably told her that he didn't want me after all, so she had to think of someplace else for me to go.

"I don't know," Fancy said. "I tried to listen at the den door, but my mother told me to cut it out."

The whole thing was pure weird. "I didn't even know the judge saw people here," I said. "He's always at his office downtown."

"He doesn't usually," Fancy said. "Only sometimes when people have to come on Saturday or if there's an emergency."

Just hearing the word *emergency* made me stop breathing. But Fancy didn't seem to notice.

Instead of counting out the money for another game, she said, "I'm sick of my stuff, and your mother said I could come to your house anytime. How about right now?"

"My mother invited you?" I asked, trying not to sound as flabbergasted as I felt. Mama must have needed a giant favor from the judge. Plus, I bet she said it just for show. And when she got home from work, she'd warn me again not to ever let a colored person in our house. Or—maybe she was setting a trap to see if I'd fall in, see if I'd go behind her back and bring Fancy home.

"She *did* invite me," Fancy said. "She even said I

should come today. Why do you sound so surprised?"

"I'm not surprised," I lied. And this *couldn't* be a trap. Mama wouldn't even be home and she never left work early so she wouldn't know if Fancy was there or not. I was worrying for nothing.

Fancy'd asked me a zillion times if we could play at my house, but I'd always managed to come up with an excuse. I felt bad about not asking her over. It was just that, besides Mama's meanness, my house was one step up from the white trash ones I'd seen in movies, and Fancy was used to so much more.

"Well, let's go," she said, excited.

"*Okay*, then. Let's go," I said, as if that's exactly what I was hoping we'd do.

"Mom! We're going to Amelia's house," Fancy yelled when we got to the bottom of the stairs. "I'll be home in a little while."

"Will her mother be there?" Mrs. Nelson called from the kitchen.

Fancy looked at me.

I shook my head no.

"Yes, she'll be there all day. You can phone and ask her if you want to."

"No, that's okay. I believe you. Have fun, but be home by five. You still have to practice your violin."

Fancy let out a tiny groan when her mother mentioned her violin. "I will."

I was so glad Mrs. Nelson didn't ask *me* about my

mother being home. I still felt guilty about the lies I'd told her when Fancy was in the judge's room. It's funny how some people make you want to be a good person.

When we got to my house, Fancy was too polite to mention anything about how shabby it was. "This is nice," she said when we walked into the kitchen. "I like that cute little table. It's like the booths they have in the soda shop."

She was talking about the old-fashioned breakfast nook by the window, the one with the cracked bench that pinches my bottom the whole time I'm eating.

She seemed sincere, so I said, "Thanks," and hurried her out of there before she noticed that we still had a sink with pipes that showed underneath and a refrigerator with the motor on top. Not to mention the speckled yellow linoleum that was worn down to a bare black path along the middle.

I didn't even stop in the living room, just headed down the hall to my room. Fancy must have sensed how embarrassed I was because she just sat on my bed and didn't mention that my room looked like an old lady must sleep there. She kept her face regular and said, "Well, what do you want to do?"

There wasn't anything *to* do. I didn't have toys. I got Christmas and birthday presents, but they were always things like pajamas or a new toothbrush—

everyday stuff most people don't have to wait a whole year for. There were leftover toys in the attic from Mama's real family, but most of them were broken and she'd warned me good not to touch Charlotte's doll collection, which I would not have wanted to do anyway since I am not the doll type. Then I remembered. "Do you want to play crazy eights?" I asked.

"Sure. That sounds like fun."

"I'll be right back," I said, relieved. I went down the hall to Grandpa Thomas's room. I hadn't been in there since he was taken away, and when I opened the door, the smell of Old Spice plowed into me so hard I had to sit on the edge of his bed until I could swallow the lump in my throat. I opened his nightstand drawer and took out the box of cards we'd played with so many times. I pressed it against my cheek and thought about how he always let me win.

As I was wiping my eyes with the cuff of my shirt, I heard a voice in the hall, not Fancy's. I opened Grandpa Thomas's door and peeked out. My mother was standing outside my bedroom, talking to Fancy!

"I see you came," she said. Her voice sounded sharp as a knife. "Would you like something to drink?" I couldn't prove it in a court of law, but I was sure that my mother *had* set a trap. And I'd fallen right into it.

"That's okay, Mama," I said fast. "I'll get us something later."

"Don't be silly," she said, way too sweet. "You two

go ahead and play. I'll bring you some of my home-made orangeade."

"Thanks, Mrs. Rye," Fancy said. "That sounds good." I could tell by the look on Fancy's face that she knew how my mother really felt about having her there—the same way she knew how Nurse Nasty felt when we were at the nursing home.

Mama passed me in the hall, and if looks were bullets, I would have been stone-cold dead.

By the time Mama came back, Fancy and I had already played two games and she was letting me win. That was the day I found out that inside that scrawny little body, she has a heart as big as Grandpa Thomas's.

"Here you go," Mama said as she handed Fancy a glass with red roses hand-painted along the rim. It was from the set she kept in the china cabinet for good, but *good* hadn't come until then. And I bet if Fancy hadn't been connected to Judge Watson, *good* still wouldn't have come. "Guests are always treated special in this house," Mama added. When I got a regular old jelly glass, Fancy gave me a look that told me she understood there was a lot about my mother that I hadn't told her.

"The judge said your mother is his housekeeper," Mama said to Fancy. "She's lucky that he gave her a job."

Fancy shot me a glance. "Yes, she is lucky," she answered, her voice plain but not rude.

I thought about Judge Watson telling people that his very own daughter was his housekeeper. It seemed to me he had his own Faith Divine—two of them, in fact.

"Well, drink your orangeade," Mama said. She stood right over Fancy and never took her eyes off that rosebud glass. Fancy held it with both hands, gulped down her drink, then handed the glass back fast.

"Thanks, Mrs. Rye," Fancy said. "That was really good."

Mama smiled, forced. Then she left without saying a word.

We'd just started our third game when Fancy said, "I have to go home. I have a lot of things to do."

I knew she was lying, but sometimes you just go along with a thing because you're relieved that the misery is almost over. And there was another thing I was sure of. Fancy would never tell her mother or Judge Watson how badly Mama had treated her because that would be the end of the road for us. And she didn't want that any more than I did.

After Fancy left, I lay on my bed, locked the whole awful afternoon away in the farthest corner of my mind, and fell asleep.

When I woke up and went down the hall, Mama sent me to the kitchen to check on supper. Next to the pot of leftover stew simmering on the stove was a pan of boiling water. Inside, bubbling away, was the glass with the red roses hand-painted along the rim.

At dinner that night, Mama gave me an extra big bowl of stew with lots of turnips because she knew how much I hated them. And when we were seated at the breakfast nook, she started in on me. "You're quite the little liar, aren't you?" she said, all satisfied with herself.

I didn't look up, just kept trying to make my stew disappear.

"Just look at your fingernails," she said. "See those white spots? Each one represents a lie you've told. That's God's way of letting people see what kind of person you are."

I looked at my hands. She couldn't possibly be right about that one. If God tallied up all the lies I'd told in my life, every one of my fingernails would be pure white.

11

Out of the mouths of babes

It's strange how you can just be in a place, minding your own business, when trouble comes and finds you. And sometimes it wears orthopedic shoes, smells like Sucrets, and teaches fifth grade in Sullivan's Falls. Miss Dumfrey'd been around so long that she knew everything about everybody—well, almost everybody, if you know what I mean. Fancy and I figured that she'd just crawled out of hell to torture people, especially if your family was not what you would call regular or if you were funny-looking or dumb or poor.

And her brother, "Chrome Dome" Dumfrey, was the principal, so she could get away with anything, even whacking us with a ruler, which she seemed to really enjoy. Of course, she didn't smack the kids whose parents would make a fuss about it. Like she never touched April Sellers, whose father was a dentist and could get her back good if she needed a filling or a tooth pulled. And David Hanson's uncle was a policeman who could throw her in the slammer. And she'd never lay a hand on her little pet, Lydia Thorngood, with her blond curls and rosy cheeks, which I am sure were fake, but I could never prove it because Lydia squealed and ran away every time I tried to get close enough to rub her face to see if the pink came off. And she left you alone if you lived with Judge Watson, even if your mother was just the maid.

When Miss Dumfrey wasn't swatting our backsides or yelling at someone to *"Shut up!"* she sat at her desk and had us read pages in our textbooks while she drank coffee from a thermos and read movie magazines. Sometimes she dozed off and no one in the class moved one tiny inch. She was a light sleeper, and when she woke up, she was even crabbier than usual. If you placed a speck of dust on the tip of your finger and then blew it away, that's how much we learned from her.

It was getting close to Christmas, and Miss Dumfrey's hand got stronger and that ruler stung even more. They say the holidays are hard on people who don't have friends or family members to share the joy of the season. As far as I could see, the other teachers were as afraid of her as we were, and I couldn't imagine old Chrome Dome decorating a tree or carving a roast goose.

It was on a Friday afternoon that Miss Dumfrey ended up getting her own whipping. I remember that for sure because every Friday the Catholic kids got out early to go to catechism, which I think is just pure unfair. A kid should not have to stay in school an extra hour just because they were born a Baptist or a Jew or, in my case, a First Redeemer. Fancy was one of the lucky ones, which meant that I had to sit behind an empty chair while she escaped to do her holy stuff.

While the Catholics were getting their coats, Miss Dumfrey instructed the rest of us to read chapter twelve in our history books—"Plymouth Plantation," which we had already read the month before, but nobody was about to point that out. The ruler was in Miss Dumfrey's hand—ready for action. She parked herself behind her desk with a mail-order catalog, the one we had at home, which featured the hot pink two-wheeler with the racing tires, wicker basket, and chrome headlight. I wanted that bike so much, but I knew I'd never get it. So I'd done the next best thing. I'd cut the picture out of the catalog, showed it to Fancy a million times, then carried it around in my pocket and looked at it whenever I wanted. That's what I was doing when the ruler cracked down on my hand. I'd been so lost in my daydream about riding the bike that I didn't even realize Miss Dumfrey and her rubber-soled shoes were headed toward the back row—and me! Usually, she went for rumps, but this time she had a different target, and she got a direct hit on skin and bones. The scream I let out sounded as if it had come from an injured animal instead of a ten-year-old girl.

She loomed over me and yelled, "What are you supposed to be doing?" Her furious voice matched the look on her face.

When I didn't answer, she raised that ruler to have a second go and said, "Hold out your hand!" Her tone was evil—like Mama's when she was at her worst.

I'd never disobeyed a teacher before, so like an idiot, I started to do what she told me to. But just as I was about to get clobbered again, I pulled my hand back. "No," I said. "I won't." It was almost a whisper. But I looked her right in the eye. The ruler smashed against my desk and broke. Half of it dropped to the floor, but the other half stayed in Miss Dumfrey's hand—all jagged and splintery like a knife. Miss Dumfrey opened her mouth to say something, but changed her mind. She stared at the ruler for a long minute and then at me. Her eyes were spitting fire, and I thought maybe she was going to stab me. Instead, she took a long, deep breath and said, "Miss Rye, you'll be keeping me company after school today. We can have a nice long talk about what just happened here."

When she headed to the front of the room, Fancy

came over, crouched down, and pretended she was searching for something in her desk. "Are you all right?" she whispered.

I kept my eyes on Miss Dumfrey's back. "I guess so," I said.

Fancy smiled at me and said, "That was the bravest thing I've ever seen."

After the catechism kids left, Miss Dumfrey said all singsong, "Well, it seems as if one of your classmates thinks she doesn't have to follow the rules. So because of her, you'll all spend the rest of the afternoon with your heads on your desks."

That was fine with me. My hand was hurting so bad I could snivel into the crook of my elbow and nobody would see me cry. Plus, I think animals have the right idea. Licking a wound with a lot of warm spit does make it feel better.

While I was worrying about what was going to happen after school, I saw the Robertson twins laughing, but the boy who sat next to me caught my eye, grinned huge, and gave me a thumbs-up. I must have looked confused, because he leaned over and whispered, "Way to go!" just like I was a regular person instead of an outcast.

A little speck of happiness nipped at my heart. But because this kind of thing had never happened before and *after school* was coming fast, I didn't smile back.

When it was time for the bell to ring, the door opened and in walked Judge Watson with Fancy right behind him.

Miss Dumfrey quickly closed the catalog and stood by her desk, smiling like butter wouldn't melt in her mouth. Judge Watson didn't even look her way, just motioned for me to come with them. While I was getting my coat, the kids gawked at me dumbstruck, as if I was Lois Lane and Superman had just flown in the door to rescue me from Lex Luthor. Sometimes a thing surprises you so much, you just go along with it and don't ask any questions.

As soon as we got outdoors, Judge Watson asked to see my hand. He laid it on his own palm and ran his fingers gently over the bruise. He was being so kind. I wondered if my daddy would have done the same, or if he would have even rescued me at all.

Judge Watson asked me to make a fist. When I did, he said, "It's not broken, but she left a heck of a welt." He shook his head and mumbled something I couldn't understand.

Then Fancy chimed in with "I think Miss Dumfrey is really Beelzebub in a stinky dress. You should have seen the look on her face while she was whopping Amelia. It was as if she was bewitched."

I was hoping Judge Watson would march right back in school and give Miss Dumfrey what-for, but he didn't. All he said was "I have some business to take care of, but first let's go downtown. I think a little ice cream might make you girls feel better."

As soon as Fancy and I were in the backseat of that long black DeSoto Firedome sedan, I started feeling a lot better. Funny how a really crummy day can turn a corner fast, the same as that spiffy car on its supersoft cushion tires.

After we had our ice cream, I asked Judge Watson to drop me off at Shady Oaks, and I found Grandpa Thomas in the dark green La-Z-Boy in the corner of the sunroom. He had a sprig of plastic holly pinned to his shirt collar, which made me feel good that somebody had cared enough to put it there. I was glad he was awake because I needed a hug. I sat on his lap, and even though I had to put his arm around me and hold it there, it was still an official hug. Every time I went to visit, I was foolish enough to think that a miracle might have taken place and he'd be able to talk to me. But that didn't happen. It was okay, though, because I'd had him whole for long enough to know what he was thinking. I just would have liked to hear his voice again.

There were a lot of people in the sunroom, more than usual, maybe because of the Christmas tree and the decorations, so I had to talk kind of loud. "Judge Watson took Fancy and me to the soda shop," I said.

Judge Watson himself?

"Yup. And we could order anything we wanted." Judge Watson didn't act what you would call grandfatherly toward Fancy, but he didn't seem embarrassed to be seen with her, so I think she was wrong about him being ashamed of her.

I bet you ordered a hot fudge sundae with whipped cream and double cherries on top.

I said, "I did," kind of cheery-like, but I had to squeeze back some tears, because Grandpa Thomas used to take me to the soda shop all the time and I hadn't been there since. "Fancy had a strawberry ice cream soda with vanilla ice cream."

That sounds good. And what about Judge Watson? I bet he just had coffee. He keeps himself pretty fit. He probably doesn't go in much for sweets.

"That's what I thought," I said. "And he did have coffee, but he had a banana split to go with it, a Pig's Dinner in a wooden trough. And he ate the whole thing."

Good for him! That's just what I would have gotten.

Then I remembered my bike picture. I reached into my coat pocket so I could show it to Grandpa Thomas, but it wasn't there. It must have fallen out when Fancy and I were horsing around in Judge Watson's car. I had every single bit of that bike memorized, so it didn't really matter. I just laid my head on my grandpa's shoulder trying to imagine what he would say.

What was the special occasion that made the judge

leave work in the middle of the day? Was it Fancy's birthday or something?

I looked down at my hand. There was still a red spot, but it only hurt if I touched it. "Miss Dumfrey walloped me good and—"

What? That miserable so-and-so hit you again? She should have been run out of that school years ago.

"Fancy skipped catechism and went and told her grandfather what happened. He came to school to make sure I was okay. Then he took us to the soda shop." I didn't want Grandpa Thomas to get more upset, so I said, "My hand's fine now. It wasn't a big deal."

But what I'd just said *was* a gigantic deal. I looked around, and Nurse Nasty was standing right behind me, holding Grandpa Thomas's pill bottle and a glass of water. And I could tell by the surprised look on her face that she'd heard every single word about Judge Watson being Fancy's grandfather.

The next day in school, we had a new teacher— young like she had just finished college. When she told us Miss Dumfrey had decided to retire, the class broke out in cheers and whistles. Fancy and I didn't join in though. We just looked at each other. We were as thrilled as everybody else, but when you have a part in another person's downfall, you do not gloat about it.

I did not tell Fancy I had broken my promise and blabbed her secret. How could I? I was afraid it would be the end of our friendship. So that new secret sat heavy in my gut like a balled-up fist. The worst part was not knowing when that fist would rise up and punch me square in the face.

The story about Fancy didn't appear in the newspaper. But it spread just as fast. In a town the size of Sullivan's Falls, it doesn't take long for news as juicy as that to get around.

"Amelia! Get out here!" Mama shrieked from the kitchen as soon as she came home from work that afternoon.

I was in my room, going over what had happened with Nurse Nasty in my head, when I heard Mama's voice. My breathing shut down, and fear kept me glued to the bed. Then I heard footsteps coming my way and my whole self froze up even more. I just hoped she'd kill me fast and not torture me first. My eyes were smash closed, but I knew she was standing over me because I could hear her wheezing, the way she did when she got herself worked up good.

She squeezed my cheeks hard against my teeth. "Look at me!" she bellowed. I managed to open one eye enough to see that her face had turned purple and her lips were clenched into a tight, straight line.

"What were you thinking, spreading that ridiculous rumor about Judge Watson?" She grabbed me by the ear and used it as a handle to pull me up off the bed, then she shook it so hard, I thought it was going to break off. "We'll be lucky if he doesn't run us out of town. Why did you lie like that? Sometimes you act like you don't have a brain in your head!"

I just stood there, looking as guilty as I felt.

"Say something, damn it!"

Up until then, my mother would have bitten her tongue off before she uttered a swearword, so I knew I'd better come up with something fast. "I was just kidding around," I said. "I didn't mean any harm."

She stared at me blank-eyed and slack-jawed. "You were just kidding around about Judge Watson being the father of a *Negro*? Why didn't you just shoot him? It would have been kinder."

Just when I thought I couldn't sound any stupider if I tried, I up and outdid myself. "I don't know," I answered. "I didn't think of that."

Even *she* couldn't come up with a reply to that one, so she just shook her head and left me standing there in the middle of my own misery.

Sometimes when a secret is let out into the open, the wind blows the stink off it. And all the worrying I did about Fancy disowning me as her friend was wasted time. On Christmas Eve Day, she called and asked me to come to her house to play and have supper.

When Fancy and I were alone in her room, she never even mentioned the fact that I had betrayed her. And after Mrs. Nelson put the food on the table, we all held hands while Judge Watson said grace. He didn't say anything about the beautiful turkey or the candied yams or the cranberry sauce. He used up the entire prayer thanking God for his daughter and his granddaughter and the memory of Fancy's granny. At the end, he looked over at me and recited a verse from the Bible—the one about *out of the mouths of babes.* Then he said, "Thank you, Amelia, for doing what I should have done a long time ago."

And on Christmas morning, he thanked me even better. When I opened the front door to put a dish of milk out for the neighbor's cat, there it was on the porch—the hot pink two-wheeler with the racing tires, wicker basket, and chrome headlight.

12

Jesus and Amelia Earhart

Can you imagine having to be baptized when you're already half grown? Mama always went to church, but she never took me. And you know how people say to count your blessings? Well, I counted not having to go to church as one of my top ten, right up there with being able to screech-whistle through my thumbs. But I guess Mama started to worry about what would happen to my soul if I got hit by a truck or she dropped over dead and whoever ended up with me was a heathen, so when Easter Sunday came around, she decided to get me baptized before either of those things happened.

When I told her I didn't want to do it, she said, "So you want to spend eternity in the fires of hell with the devil poking you in the backside with his pitchfork?"

"That doesn't sound so bad," I said. "We could roast

marshmallows." After Mama'd had her conniption about me making up lies concerning Judge Watson, and nobody—especially Judge Watson—made much of a to-do about it, some of the wind seemed to go out of her sails. Even better, I'd had a growth spurt and she was going the other way. I was taller than she was and I could run faster, so I started to get a little bit sassy. I knew where to draw the line, though, because I still needed a place to live and I liked to eat, but it was fun to see her simmer. "I'm just kidding," I said. "But I don't see how having a few drops of water sprinkled on my head is going to save my soul."

She looked at me as if I was the biggest idiot she'd ever met. "It's not regular water," she said, annoyed. "It's special because it's put there by a holy man."

"I know," I said. "I just think I'm too old for this."

"Nobody's ever too old to become a child of God," she said, all high and mighty. "And it's the only way you'll be reunited with your family in heaven."

"Oh, good," I said. "Maybe I'll get to see William pitch another fit."

She shook her head and rolled her eyes. "You'd better watch your mouth or you'll end up eating ashes with the devil tonight instead of my baked ham and scalloped potatoes."

She had me there. She made the best ham and scalloped potatoes in the entire world and I didn't want to miss that meal.

The church was decorated with Easter lilies and filled to overflowing with people who only showed up once a year. Mama and I were parked in the middle of the second row. She had me gussied up good in a hideous white nylon dress Sylvia'd worn a million Easters ago. Every inch of that thing had a bow or a ribbon or a plastic rhinestone sewn on it. And the nylon was so slippery I had to keep my feet planted firmly on the floor so I didn't shoot right off that polished wooden pew.

Just before the service started, a woman wearing a fox stole sat down in front of me. I don't know anything about fur, but I could tell it was a fox because it had a fox's head, fox feet with real fox toenails, and even a genuine fox tail. It was curled around the woman's neck with its head resting on its tail, and its yellow glass eyes were looking straight at me. When I leaned forward to get a closer look at those eyes, Sylvia's nylon dress got a mind of its own, slid sideways, and sent me to the floor. On the way down, my nose clipped the back of the fox woman's pew, so when Mama yanked me back up, the front of that dress looked as if somebody had just slit my throat. She slapped a handkerchief over my face and whispered, "Pinch your nose with this and don't you make one single sound." Then she took off her old-lady sweater and told me to put it on and button it.

We stood up and sat down a thousand times, sang a bunch of hymns that didn't rhyme, and listened to a drawn-out sermon about how Jesus died on the cross so all of us sinners could go to heaven. I was sorry Jesus had to go through all that awful stuff for me, but I really couldn't think of anything I'd done that was so bad, except maybe the time I swiped a pack of gum from the drugstore. But even then, I felt so guilty I went back and left a nickel on the counter when the clerk wasn't looking. I figured Jesus's suffering might have been better spent on somebody else—a thief, maybe, or a murderer.

After the collection, the preacher asked the parents of the children who were to be baptized to bring them to the altar. Three young couples stood up with brand-new babies. My stomach twisted into a knot and I leaned toward Mama. "Please don't make me do this," I said. "It's too embarrassing and my nose hurts bad."

She whispered, "Your nose is your own doing and I'm not bringing you back here again, so let's go." She stood up and motioned for me to follow.

I didn't.

She motioned again, harder.

I stayed where I was and concentrated on that fox's leather nose.

Then the preacher stuck *his* nose in. "Come along, Mrs. Rye," he said. "And bring—" He looked down at a paper he was holding. "Bring Amelia Earhart with you."

Sometimes, when you think a situation can't get any worse, it does. Now every eye in the place was on Mama, and they were all waiting for Amelia Earhart to rise from the dead, just like Jesus.

I rose, but when I did, I headed the other way, right up the aisle and out the door.

By the time Mama got home, I'd changed out of that ugly dress and stuffed it into the trash can near the kitchen door so she couldn't miss it. When she came into my room, I was sitting on my bed, reading *A Tree Grows in Brooklyn*, my favorite book ever.

"I hope you're proud of yourself," Mama said, all dramatic.

"I am," I answered, without looking up.

I waited for her to grab the book out of my hand and give me a lecture about how I'd embarrassed her and was going to hell for sure because I hadn't been baptized. But all she said was "You'll stay in your room for the rest of the day with no lunch. You can come out when it's time for supper."

"No, thanks," I said.

Mama's tone turned haughty. "What do you mean— *no thanks*? I said you're *not* to leave this room."

"I'll stay here," I said, still not looking at her. "But no thanks to supper."

Out of the corner of my eye, I saw her shift from one foot to the other. Then she cleared her throat slow, as if she didn't know what to do with me. "Of *course* you'll have supper," she said, halfway nice. "You *love* my ham and scalloped potatoes."

"No, I don't. Your ham's always dry and the potatoes taste like paste."

"But you've always said it's your favorite." Her voice was high and thin.

I held my hand in the air and pointed to my fingernail. "Well, that's probably the lie that caused this white spot right here."

A sigh rolled out of her mouth that sounded like an old car trying to start up. "You'll stay in your room for the rest of the day, and when I call you for supper, I expect you to come. Do you understand?"

I nodded. "I understand." Just thinking about that juicy ham and those delicious potatoes made my mouth water. And the apple pie Mama was going to bake would beat Betty Crocker's any day.

After she left, I closed my door, crawled out my window, jumped on my beautiful bike, and headed to Shady Oaks to wish Grandpa Thomas a happy Easter.

13

Miracles, saints, and stuff about my daddy

The next day, when I walked into Grandpa Thomas's room, there was Margo LaRue, cutting his hair and singing "What a Friend We Have in Jesus." She'd gotten a job as the nursing home hairdresser, and she was all toned down in the hubba-hubba department—regular-length skirt, buttoned-up blouse, and hardly any makeup. I think the boss of Shady Oaks made her wash her face and keep all her sexy accessories strapped down, so the old men wouldn't have heart attacks. I almost didn't recognize her except for her gentle voice and egg-yolk-colored curls. I tried to duck out fast before she saw me, but no dice.

"Well, hi there, honey," she said, and then she got red in the face. "I don't usually sing in public, but these older folks are partial to hymns, so I do the best I can to entertain them while I work."

She was really a pretty good singer, but hymns were the last thing Grandpa Thomas was partial to. Grandma Nellie'd shoved religion down his throat for so long he nearly choked to death, and then Mama took over with *her* holier-than-thou ways. "I'm actually looking forward to going to hell," he told me one day when Mama'd gotten on his case again about his gambling. "At least down there I won't have to listen to a bunch of hypocrites tell me how evil I am. I'll look around till I find some of my old cronies. We'll set up a card game and get ourselves a bottle of hooch and have a good old time." That was when I decided that hell was where I wanted to end up, too. Grandpa Thomas had already taught me how to play poker, so I was all set in that department. My drink will be Dr Pepper, but I plan to go wherever he goes.

Margo LaRue tilted her head to one side. "You're Fancy's little friend, right? Long time no see." She pointed her scissors at Grandpa Thomas. "Are you here to visit Mr. Rye?"

Now *that's* how a lie snakes around and bites you straight in the behind. Just as I was about to say I was in the wrong room, a nurse came in and said, "Hi, Amelia, your grandpa's getting the royal treatment today. Doesn't he look nice?"

I glanced at Margo LaRue. Her smile melted, and a fog crept over her face. "Didn't you tell me your last name is Earhart?" she asked.

The nurse was standing behind me. She put her hands on my shoulders and rocked me back and forth a little. "This is Amelia Rye," she said. "She comes to see her grandfather every day." Then she turned me around so she could look into my eyes. "I think that's why he's beginning to get better."

I stared at her, dumbfounded. "What do you mean?" I asked. "I didn't think he'd *ever* get any better."

She smiled and shrugged her shoulders. "He moved his right index finger in therapy today, so that's a good sign."

"*He did?*" Most people wouldn't think moving a finger was anything to get excited about, but she might as well have told me that Grandpa Thomas had gotten up and danced the jitterbug. I hugged that nurse so tight and for such a long time, she finally had to pry my arms away so she could breathe.

"We don't know how much he'll improve," she added. "Or if he'll go back to where he was. But sometimes miracles *do* happen." Her voice cracked. "And—well—I just think you're helping this one along." When she patted my cheek, her hand smelled like baby powder with a little bit of rubbing alcohol tossed in. "Now I have to go," she said. "I just stopped in to tell you the good news."

"Well, I'm real happy for you, Amelia," Margo LaRue said. "And for Mr. Rye, too. I hope he keeps on getting better." She did not look straight at me and she did not mention the lie I'd told her when I was in Fancy's kitchen. She just got back to cutting Grandpa Thomas's hair.

I pulled a straight-back chair over next to Grandpa Thomas and put my hand on his arm. "The nurse told me you're getting better," I said. "I'm glad."

Because Margo LaRue was there, I couldn't concentrate enough to imagine what he might say back, so I just sat and watched her do her job.

But then she said, "Mr. Rye, why don't you show us what you can do with your finger?"

She stopped cutting, and we both stared at Grandpa Thomas's hand—nothing. My heart sank, and I thought the nurse must have made a mistake. It was somebody else's grandfather who'd gotten the miracle.

"Go ahead, Mr. Rye," Margo LaRue said. "Show us how you can move that finger." She stood next to him and wiggled her own finger in front of his face.

Grandpa Thomas stayed still as a rock.

I took his hand in mine and said, "That's okay. You don't have to do it if you don't want to." Then it happened—I felt his finger press against the palm of my hand. I was so filled with joy that the dam in my heart busted wide open and a flood of happy tears poured down my face.

"Oh, honey," Margo LaRue said, reaching out to pat

my head. "Don't cry. Maybe he just doesn't feel like doing it any more today."

"Yeah, maybe," I sobbed. I wiped my face with the Kleenex she handed me. "That's probably it." But *I* knew what was going on. Grandpa Thomas wasn't about to perform for the woman who'd lured his son away from his family. And I wasn't going to share his accomplishment with her either.

"You just keep your hopes up, sweetie," Margo LaRue said. "And I'll be rooting for you both." She took the towel off Grandpa Thomas's shoulders and shook it over the wastebasket. "Well, I'm done here. I'll get out of your way so you two can have a nice visit."

As she was leaving, she turned around and looked back at me. "Amelia," she said, all serious. "I only have one more haircut to do. Would it be all right if I come back when I'm finished and give you a ride home? I have something I want to talk to you about."

That was the last thing I expected her to say, so I just sat there like a dope. But then I felt Grandpa Thomas's finger against my hand again and I said, "Sure. That'll be okay." He must have wanted to know what she had to say as much as I did.

When we were alone, I asked Grandpa Thomas to move his finger again, so I could actually see it. He tapped the arm of the chair three times, slow and deliberate.

Then I remembered Fancy's Magic 8 Ball. "Grandpa Thomas," I said. "Tap once for yes, twice for no, and three times for I don't know, okay?"

He tapped once.

My mind was so overloaded with the excitement of the whole thing, I couldn't think of anything sensible to ask him, even though I'd been waiting for this to happen for a whole year. "Is it sunny out?"

Three taps. My breath caught in my throat. Maybe he was blind. Then I woke up and realized that the window was behind him. "Oh, sorry," I said. "I'll try another one. Is my middle name Earhart?"

Tap.

"Are you hungry or anything?"

Tap, tap.

"Okay, good, it works. Isn't that great?"

Tap. A little stronger this time.

I expected him to be smiling like me, but his face was still plain. That's when I realized that maybe this was about as far as he'd ever get and we'd have to be happy with little victories. But nobody had expected even this much, so anything was possible. And just knowing that he was still in there was enough for me.

The inside of Margo LaRue's car was a royal wreck, like the city dump had exploded and nobody bothered to clean it up. She had to clear a pile of junk off the passenger seat so I'd have a place to sit. She didn't even seem embarrassed, just kept tossing Avon catalogs, hairbrushes, gum wrappers, magazines, even a half-used tube of toothpaste into the backseat. Then she picked up a yellow plastic kazoo with the word *Revlon* printed on it. "They gave these out at a hair show I went to a few years ago, but I don't know how to play it." She handed it to me. "Maybe you do."

I thought everybody knew how to play a kazoo. "All you do is hum into it," I said, holding it out to give it back.

She shook her head. "I'm no good with musical instruments. Why don't you give it a try?"

At first I couldn't think of anything to play, but then the news about Grandpa Thomas started to sink in, and it made me want to celebrate. "I'll play my grandfather's favorite," I said. "'When the Saints Go Marching In.'"

"I just love that song," Margo LaRue said, motioning for me to get in the car.

I started out slow, but Margo LaRue began to clap, so I followed along and picked up the beat.

When I was finished, she said, "You're really good!"

"Thanks," I said, a little embarrassed, because what I'd done was nothing.

As soon as Margo LaRue was behind the wheel, she said, "I was hoping we could go to my apartment and have a bite to eat. Do you think that would be okay with your mother?"

When I woke up that morning and thought about the things I was going to do, eating lunch in Margo LaRue's apartment was not one of them. "She wouldn't mind," I said. She wouldn't mind because I sure wasn't going to tell her about it.

Once we were on our way, I thought maybe Margo LaRue would at least give me a hint about why she wanted to talk to me, but instead, she started singing "The Saints," and I joined in with the kazoo. By the time we were parked in her driveway, we were experts. "Let's do it again," she said. This time I started it off with a screech whistle and played extra loud. She sang and used the steering wheel as a bongo drum.

When we finished, she laughed, hard. "Oh, that was fun!" she choked. "I can't remember when I had such a good time."

It's strange how she could make a kid feel like a regular person. But it was sad in a way, kind of like other adults didn't want anything to do with her, so she made friends with kids and other outsiders.

The apartment turned out to be one tiny room with a kitchenette, bathroom down the hall—almost as messy as her car. I was trying to figure out where she slept when she reached up, turned a knob on the wall, and down came a bed, complete with sheets and a blanket. "Have you ever seen one of these?" she asked.

"Never!" I said, shaking my head. She was like one of those magicians on *The Ed Sullivan Show*.

She sat on the edge and bounced up and down a few times. "It's called a Murphy bed. They're for people who live in matchboxes, like me."

I wondered why she didn't have a real apartment. As far as I knew, now that she worked at Shady Oaks, she had three jobs. That should have given her plenty of money to rent a decent-size place. I didn't have to wonder long. As she was patting the bed for me to sit down next to her, she said, "One of these days I'll be able to buy a little house of my own. As soon as I save up enough money."

"That would be nice," I said, lame. I wished so much that Fancy was with us. It was okay in the car with the kazoo to keep us occupied, but now the mood had changed and I was pretty much tongue-tied.

Then Margo LaRue said, "I need to tell you something, and as much as you might want to leave, I'd like you to stay until I have it all out. Do you think you can do that?"

The whole thing was giving me a bad case of the jitters. "I'll try," I answered. I moved a little bit away from her. Was she going to tell me about my daddy? Fear whirled around inside my head and made me feel so queasy, I started counting again. *One, two, three, four, five, six, seven.*

"Before I left Sullivan's Falls," she began, "I had just opened my own beauty parlor and I was starting to build up a nice list of regulars." She lowered her eyes. "Then I met a man." She looked at me. "But you already knew that part, didn't you?"

I nodded, bit the inside of my cheek.

"I cut men's hair in the back room, and one day he came in for a haircut. He told me his name was John Rye. I already knew who he was, but I didn't let on. I joked around with him and called him Hollywood John because he was wearing sunglasses and was dressed up all spiffy in a tie."

Until that very minute, I hadn't known my daddy's first name. Mama always called him something vile, and Grandpa Thomas referred to him as his son or my father. "Why did he come to you to have his hair cut?" I asked. "I thought men went to barbershops."

She got a faraway look in her eyes, and I think she took a quick trip down memory lane before she said, "Well, he had a doozy of a shiner and his ear was all busted up. I guess he didn't want to go to the barbershop and get ribbed about how he'd been in a fight, being a preacher and all. And, well, I guess somebody must have told him about my back room."

"Did he say who beat him up?" I asked. Mama didn't tell me she'd given him a black eye when she found out she was pregnant with me.

"He said he'd been attacked by a drunk in an alley. But I don't think that's what happened. He really didn't want to talk about it, so I left it alone."

My insides were getting shakier, so I concentrated on the white spots on my fingernails. Then I asked a safe question. "What did he look like?"

She took in a big breath and let it out slow, then rubbed her thumb easy over her lips. "He was very handsome—like a movie actor. And he had blue eyes—the same as yours." She took hold of my chin, tipped it up, and stared into my eyes as if she was in a trance. "They're more than blue," she said. "They're kaleidoscope blue—like sparkling bits of glass. You're going to drive the boys crazy with those eyes some-day."

I tried to smile. Couldn't.

She let go of my chin, shook her head, and sighed. "It was his eyes that got me that day in the shop. They held me captive until I forced myself to look away. And he wasn't like any preacher I'd ever met before."

"What *was* he like?" I asked. "He was so much older than you."

"He was the same age my father would have been if he had lived," she said, pleasant, as if she hadn't noticed my high-and-mighty tone. "But he didn't seem old, just sad."

I'd never heard about my daddy being sad, only what Mama called foolish—like the time he went fish-ing and left a mess of perch in the hot car to rot. "It took six months and a king's ransom in baking soda and vinegar to get the stink out," she'd told me.

"Sometimes that man didn't have the sense God gave a gnat."

"And he was kind," Margo LaRue continued. "I can imagine what people say behind my back. That I wear too much makeup, and I bleach my hair, and my clothes are too revealing. But that's who I am and I'm not going to change for anybody." She looked down at her covered-up self. "Well, unless there's a job involved." She glanced over at me and laughed a little. "I really *do* want that house. Anyway, John said he liked me just the way I was. He complimented me about how I looked. And he listened to me when I talked as if what I had to say was important."

I remembered what Mama had told me—more times than I wanted to hear. "That man just ignored me," she said. "I'd tell him to do one thing and he'd do just the opposite. It was as if he was playing deaf on purpose."

By then I had the picture. Mama was—well—Mama. And Margo LaRue—wasn't.

My insides riled up good, and I said in an ugly voice, "You must have known he was married. Why didn't you just leave him alone?"

She let me hang on to my anger and said, "John told me that things weren't going well between your mama and him—that it was time for him to leave."

I already knew that part, so I didn't say anything.

"I had a little money saved up and a brand-new car, so John thought we should break it in by going clear across the country to San Diego."

I thought about Mama. As far as I knew, she'd never even left Sullivan's Falls.

"I got a job right away, but your father said he needed time to come to grips with what had happened between him and your mother. Besides, he wanted to find himself. All those years behind the pulpit had disguised who he really was. So while I was working, he spent his time at the beach," she said with anger in her voice. "I'm not sure if he found himself, but he sure didn't find a job, and I got tired of supporting him, so things between us fell apart pretty fast."

Serves you right is what I was thinking.

"We'd only been in California a month when he came home and told me he was moving out—that he'd been nagged enough in his life and didn't need me on his back."

There was a long minute of silence, so I looked over to see if she was going to say anything else.

She shrugged. "That's all there is. I haven't seen or heard from him since."

We both just sat on that magic bed and looked at the floor. I guess she thought I should be the one to decide when the conversation was over, which was considerate of her because I wasn't done yet. "Did you stay in California all those years?" I asked. I bet she was hoping my father would go back to her.

She shook her head. "No. I left right away. But I was too embarrassed to return to Sullivan's Falls."

I was starting to feel a little bit sorry for her. "So where did you go?"

"Just from town to town until enough time had passed that I thought maybe the people in Sullivan's Falls might have forgotten about me. My roots are here. I wanted to come home. And I was right. People have been nice to me." She smiled. "Of course, I never get to hear their second song."

"Second song? What's that?"

"It's what people say about you when you're not around to hear."

I nodded. I knew exactly what she was talking about.

Margo LaRue's face turned really serious, and she looked square at me. "I just wanted to tell you how sorry I am for ripping your family apart. And that if I'd known about you, known that your mama was pregnant, I never would have done what I did."

I didn't say, "That's okay," because it wasn't. Instead, I just looked at her for a long time, and then I said, "Daddy should have told you about me." I wondered why he didn't. Did he think a baby only belonged with its mother? But now that I was a grown-up girl, wouldn't he want to be with me?

Margo LaRue shook her head and sighed. "You're very special, Amelia. And your father sure is missing a lot by not knowing you."

Things were starting to get gooey, so I said, "Did you say something about having a bite to eat? I'm starving."

"Me, too," Margo LaRue said. She stood up and headed for the kitchenette.

The whole story had left me feeling hollow inside. But I guess sometimes, when the layers of a mystery have been stripped away, what you end up with is not nearly as dramatic as you thought it would be.

After I left Margo LaRue's apartment, I took my brother's old, rusty wagon down to the grassy embankments by the railroad tracks and searched for empties—two cents for the small beer bottles, five cents for quarts—and scrap metal for the man who ran the junkyard—ten cents a pound. I've never, to this day, told Fancy about trolling the tracks. Some things you don't tell even your best friend. But on Saturday afternoons, my trash cash got me into the movies, the same as the kids whose mamas paid their way.

14

Defending Fancy

"That was a close one!" I told Fancy as she plopped down next to me. As soon as she came to Sullivan's Falls, I started taking the school bus again. You get brave when you have a friend. Plus, those horrible Robertson twins had been thrown off the bus permanently, so we were pretty much left alone. Fancy was the last one on, and I saved her a seat, which was easy because nobody else ever sat next to me.

"I thought I was going to miss it," she said, out of breath. She was even later than usual and really had to hustle because the driver was about to give up on her and leave.

"What's that?" I asked. She had a small, soft, suitcase-like thing balanced on her lap.

"It's my ballet stuff. My lessons start after school today."

"I thought your mother took you to Montreal for ballet."

"Yeah, she used to. But guess what? There's a ballet teacher who moved here from New York City. My mom took me to meet her on Saturday."

"So what's your outfit look like?" I asked, all interested. "Is it one of those pouffy-out-skirt things?"

"Nah," she said, shaking her head. "We only wear tutus in recitals." She patted the case. "This is just my practice stuff."

Even that sounded like fun. "Can I see it?"

"Sure."

While she was unzipping the case, I thought how I'd always wanted to take ballet. I loved watching the famous ballerinas on TV with their straight backs and long legs, loved the way they floated across the stage like elegant white doves. And how their hair was always twisted into a tight knot, the classy-lady style.

As Fancy lifted a little pile of cotton-candy pink out of her case, I looked across the aisle and saw that T. F. Corrigan was watching us. He'd only been in our school a few weeks, but he'd already become the third meanest kid in the fifth grade. He didn't say anything, just kept staring. But as soon as the bus stopped in front of the school, that little wart stole Fancy's dance clothes and hightailed it. Before you could count to one, Fancy grabbed her case and took off after him.

By the time I caught up with them, T.F. had Fancy's

tights on his head—like a pink wig with long, flowy braids—and was running around the playground, swinging her leotard in the air. He looked at the gathering crowd of kids and yelled, "Hey, everybody, I've got Frances Nelson's underwear!"

T.F. was fast. But Fancy was even faster. She caught up to him, jumped on his back, wrapped her legs around his waist, and smacked his arm with her ballet case. When he started hopping like a kangaroo, she lost her grip and dropped to the ground—hard. The kids who were watching pointed and laughed. Fancy just sat there—stunned—while T.F. danced around her.

At first, all I did was stand and stare, rooted to the earth like a tree. But like Grandpa Thomas said, "All you need in life is one true friend." And right that minute, Fancy needed that friend.

I was on that little Corrigan brat before he knew what was happening. I was a lot taller than he was and stronger than I ever knew. I got him to the ground, and as he squirmed, he let loose a string of the bloodcurdling curse words he was so famous for.

The kids watching were silent for a tiny second, and then they started laughing again—this time at T.F. He'd bullied most of them, so I guess they were glad he was getting a taste of what it felt like. I started hearing things like "Punch him in the nose!" and "That'll show him!" and, best of all, "I guess Corrigan's not so tough after all if a girl can beat him up!" When T.F. heard the teasing, he squirmed even harder and turned his cursing up a notch—started yelling the industrial-strength swears.

While I held T.F. down, I called to Fancy, "Come get your stuff so I can get off this little creep." I was taking a chance with the little creep part because T.F. was the type to sneak up and knock the books out of your hands or knee you in the backside just for the fun of it. But I got carried away by the attention of the crowd. And the getting off part was giving me a case of the jitters. As long as I had him down, I was safe, like when you have a snake by the head. But when I let him loose, I wasn't looking forward to being killed.

"You big show-off," Fancy said as she pulled her tights off T.F.'s head. Then she grabbed her leotard out of his hand. "And my name's Fancy, not Frances." She patted me on the shoulder. Then she got right down in T.F.'s face. "If you call me Frances again, I'll sic my friend Amelia on you, and *then* you'll be sorry."

My heart felt proud that Fancy was bragging about me. But my brain wished she'd shut up. Threatening T.F. with me was like poking a growling dog with a feather. He had all kinds of mean moves, but all I could do was sit on him, and I was pretty sure he wasn't going to give me the chance to get him down again.

Before I let him up, I took off my glasses and gave

them to Fancy. The last thing I wanted to do was to tell Mama I'd gotten in a fight at school and busted them. I knew I couldn't outrun T.F., so I quick got up and stepped back. My hands flew to my face as I waited for the punch. But instead of getting pummeled, I smelled peanut butter and heard T.F. whisper, "I'll get you for this, Rye, you bug-eyed freak. And I'll get your little friend Frances, too. You just wait."

I let out the breath I'd been holding as T.F. headed toward the back door of the school so he didn't have to walk by the kids who were taunting him. That was when I realized bullies do their dirty work when they get you alone. That crowd was full of regular kids, but there were a lot of them—a bully's worst nightmare.

The kids who'd been watching the show stood aside to let Fancy and me go by. Nobody said anything, but the girl the mean kids called Fat Betty touched my arm and smiled at me. I smiled back. Then the pride I felt was squashed by the memory of T.F.'s threat. I knew I was going to have to pay for what I'd just done—and it would be with interest.

15

The willow pond

Fifth grade was over and school was out for the summer. It was blazing hot. Fancy and I were headed to the willow pond at the end of her street to cool off. We were wearing our bathing suits and we each had on one of her roller skates that we were using like a scooter.

As we were about to cross the road to get to the pond, the Robertson twins and T. F. Corrigan nearly ran us over with their bikes. Fancy and I had been talking and laughing so much that we hadn't heard them coming. They had towels draped around their necks and were riding in the direction of the Sullivan's Falls beach, which is about a mile and a half down the road.

Even though T.F. was small and not nearly as tough, the Robertsons had taken him on as their toady. I think in the twins' eyes, three was enough for a gang—the Mashers, a name as dumb as they were. They spent most of their time tormenting regular-acting boys—especially ones who wore glasses or braces or read books just for the fun of it. And mostly they didn't hit girls. Other than sticks-and-stones insults, they hadn't been much of a problem for Fancy and me. T.F. had never carried out his threat to get me for that day on the playground. I guess he had more important kids to torture.

The Mashers had seen Fancy and me on our way to the willow pond lots of times before, but they'd always ignored us. This time they didn't. "Hey, Frances," Eddie called as he rode by. "That's some suntan you got there."

"Thanks," Fancy answered. "I'm a Coppertone girl."

I'd told Fancy what Grandpa Thomas used to say when I was little and complained about being teased—"Fire won't burn if you don't give it fuel." He was right. It can't be fun if your victim agrees with you.

"What about you, Rye?" Jake said. "I see you're still taking those ugly pills."

"Yup," I answered back. "A double dose, twice a day."

Jake and Eddie laughed, then pedaled away, leaving T.F. behind. He looked miffed but took off after them. "See ya later, losers," he called back.

Just to make sure they were really finished with us, Fancy and I followed them with watchdog eyes until they were out of sight. As soon as they disappeared, she skated ahead to the pond and yelled, "Same as always, nobody here."

The pond wasn't much more than a gigantic puddle surrounded by willow trees, but it was cool there. We had our skates off and were splashing each other when Fancy stopped and said, "Who's that?"

"Who's who?" I answered. "I don't see anybody."

She pointed to the trees on the other side of the pond. "I thought I saw somebody over there."

"It was probably just a dog or something. Anyway, whatever it was it's gone now," I said, and we started splashing again.

Suddenly they were on us. The Mashers! Jake held my arms behind me so I couldn't get away while Eddie pushed Fancy face-first in the dirt then pinned the middle of her back down with his knee. "Come on, Corrigan," he yelled. "Let's get this over with."

I knew about the disgusting things bad boys did to girls. And all I could see were Fancy's bare legs flailing around. The fear about what was going to happen barreled into me with such force that I could hardly stand it. I struggled as much as I could, but Jake just laughed, holding me at arm's length, so I couldn't kick him.

As I squirmed, helpless, Eddie yelled at Fancy to

stop moving. Then T.F. knelt beside her, reached into his pocket, and pulled out a jackknife. *Oh my God*, I thought. *He's going to kill her.* I started screaming. Jake got red-face mad and told me to quit it or I'd be sorry.

But then T.F. began hacking away at Fancy's braids and tossing them along the shore.

"Let me go!" I hollered. I wriggled one arm free, but Jake grabbed me around the waist and slapped his other hand over my mouth—hard.

"Shut up!" he said. He was squeezing me so tight I thought my ribs were breaking.

Fancy lay motionless. I watched as everything got eerie quiet. There wasn't a sound except for the whisper of the wind moving through the willow leaves and the slicing noise that knife made as it cut through Fancy's hair.

I couldn't move or call out, so I started counting in my head, only this time it was different. The numbers came slow and heavy like angry beats on a bass drum, and the counting didn't block out what was happening, just made it seem worse.

"Done!" T.F. said as he closed his knife and shoved it in his pocket. He stood up and looked at me. "I told you I'd get back at you, Rye."

I guess T.F. figured the best way to torture me was to hurt Fancy, and I wondered how a person like him would know a thing like that.

When Jake finally loosened his grip, I bolted toward T.F. He tripped me, then ripped my glasses off and threw them against a tree.

"Okay. We did what we came for," Jake announced. "Let's get outta here." He looked down at Fancy and me. "You keep your mouths shut and we'll leave you alone. As far as I can see, you and Corrigan are fair and square." Then he looked at T.F. and added, "You better have that money for us. My stomach's growling already for a hot dog and a milk shake."

And then—just like that—they were gone.

Seeing Fancy just lying there with her braids scattered all around her made my heart bust wide open. And then tears came—huge, stinging tears. "Are you okay?" I asked.

She nodded a little and started to get up.

I touched her arm, then helped her crawl over to the trunk of a willow tree. We leaned our backs against it and watched heavy gray clouds bury the sun.

Fancy drew her knees to her chest, wrapped her arms around them, then rocked back and forth, staring at the ground. The mud on her cheek had dried gray, and she was trying to wipe it away. There was a desperate hurt in her eyes. "Even the white kids in Alabama never treated me *that* bad," she said with disbelief in her voice.

There were no more words. I looked down at my pale arms and felt ashamed. I didn't know what to say and I didn't think Fancy wanted to talk about it any-more. As we sat there, it started to rain—hard.

Fancy stood up. "I want to go home now," she announced.

I went over and got my glasses, which were still in one piece, if you didn't count the fact that a side part was cracked and hanging by a broken screw. Then I walked along the shore and picked up each and every one of Fancy's braids. I handed them to her.

She stared at them. "They made me look like a baby. I've wanted to cut those things off for years, but my mother wouldn't let me." She rubbed her hand over her head. "I'm just not sure I want my hair to be *this* short."

As I struggled to keep my glasses from falling off, Fancy tried to straighten them, but it was hopeless. "I'm sorry about these, too," she said. "If you hadn't stuck up for me the day T.F. stole my ballet stuff, they wouldn't have gotten busted."

"It's okay," I said. "Now my mother'll have to buy me a decent pair." I knew that wasn't going to happen, but I didn't want Fancy to feel any worse than she already did.

Neither of us felt like skating, so we walked to her house barefoot. When we were almost there, Fancy said, "Will you go ahead and see where my mother is?"

"Sure," I said. "But what if she asks me where you are?"

"Just say you're thirsty and you came back for a drink of water." She looked over at me with her bleak face. "I can't tell her what happened back there. She'd never let me out of her sight again."

"But she's gonna know—"

"Just *do* it—okay? I have a plan, but I need your help."

Any other time I would have told her to cut out the bossy attitude. But right then, I was just happy that the old sassy-mouthed Fancy was still alive and kicking in that skinny little body. I handed her the skate I was carrying. "I'll be right back."

I didn't have to go far because Mrs. Nelson was sitting on the front porch, reading a book. I ran back and told Fancy.

"Did she see you?" Fancy asked, worried.

"No, she didn't even look up."

"Okay, good. We'll go in the back door."

"Hi, Mrs. Nelson," I said when I stepped out onto the porch. "Fancy'd like you to come inside. She wants to show you something. It's a surprise."

"Oh, hi, Amelia," she said in her usual upbeat voice. "When did you two get back? I didn't hear you come in." I'd patched up my broken glasses with adhesive tape from her medicine cabinet, but she was too polite to mention how strange they looked.

"Well, we didn't want to disturb your reading and we were all wet so we just went around to the back."

"I'm not sure I'm up for one of Fancy's surprises today," Mrs. Nelson said as she was opening the door to go in. She looked at me—serious. "She's not going to jump out of a closet and scare me, is she? I swear if that child does that again, I'll drop dead on the spot."

I shook my head. "She's not going to jump out of anywhere."

"Well, then," she said, relieved. "It can't be that bad. Where is she?"

"She's in the bathroom off the kitchen."

When Mrs. Nelson saw Fancy standing at the sink holding a pair of scissors, she clamped her hands over her mouth. "Dear God in heaven! What have you gone and done now?" Her voice was stretched tight, and the vein in the side of her neck stuck out so far I thought it was going to burst wide open.

Fancy's braids, with the barrettes still attached, lay in a heap on the toilet seat. She patted her hair, then turned to her mom. "Don't you think it looks nice?" she asked, all soft and innocent.

Mrs. Nelson just stood there, opening and closing her mouth like a goldfish. Finally, when she got words to come out, she said, "Frances Marguerite Nelson! It looks as if somebody attacked your hair with a hatchet. What in the world were you thinking?"

Fancy blinked hard, then looked down at the hair in the sink that was left after we tried to even up the mess. "I don't know," she sobbed. I wasn't sure if she was acting or if the horror of what happened earlier was just sinking in. "I wanted a change."

"Well, you got one all right," Mrs. Nelson said. But then she did the strangest thing—she started to laugh. She wrapped her arms around Fancy and laughed like the funniest thing in the world had just happened. And then Fancy joined in.

That's when I realized that as long as Fancy—and girls like her—had their mamas, the sharp edges of their lives would always be smoothed out for them. A terrible, jealous anger rose up in me, and suddenly I didn't feel one bit sorry for Fancy anymore. I would have shaved my head bald if I could have had a mother like hers.

16

Just like Audrey Hepburn

ancy and I spent the rest of the summer in her back yard, playing badminton and running under the hose. Neither of us has mentioned what happened at the willow pond—ever. Talking about it would make it real. Mrs. Nelson questioned us about it a few times, but when we told her we were tired of going there, she dropped it. That summer I learned secrets are a big part of the glue that binds two souls together forever.

When August came, Fancy's hair had grown out pretty good, so Mrs. Nelson asked Margo LaRue to come to the house to style it.

"You look so grown-up," Margo LaRue told Fancy when she was finished.

And she did. Those braids were cute when she was younger, but now she looked as if she was wearing a soft black crown.

"The short cut really brings out your eyes," Mrs. Nelson said, smiling.

She was right. Fancy has these amazing dark eyes that look wet all the time.

"I like it," Fancy said after she looked in the mirror. "Thanks, Miss LaRue."

"You're very welcome, sweetie. You just let me know when you need a trim."

As she was packing up her stuff, she looked over at me and said, "Amelia, would *you* like a haircut?" She pointed to her bag on the kitchen table. "I've got everything I need right here and I have plenty of time."

"I think we should ask her mother first," Mrs. Nelson said fast.

"Oh, we don't have to do that," I said, even faster. "She wouldn't mind. She's planning to take me for one soon anyway," which was a bald-faced lie. I'd never had a professional haircut in my life. Every once in a while, Mama'd get out her sewing shears and even up the bottom, but that was it.

And the part about asking Mama if Margo LaRue could cut my hair—well—Mama'd probably send me to live with my brother, Jack, in prison just because I'd talked to Margo. She'd never once mentioned the fact that Margo LaRue was back in town even though she must have seen her by then. And Margo LaRue had never said anything about running into my mother. I guess grownups send unpleasant things like that to the darkest corners of their minds and hope they die there.

"Okay then," Mrs. Nelson said, "I'll leave you ladies alone. I've got a pile of school clothes to hem."

She was right about that. Judge Watson had driven Fancy and her mother to Albany for the weekend and they came home with a slew of new outfits for Fancy. They even brought me one—a dusty blue skirt with a matching lamb's wool sweater. It was my first brand-new outfit ever and so beautiful that I was actually looking forward to school so I could wear it.

When I took the clothes home, Mama said the same thing she said when Judge Watson gave me my Christmas bike, "Be sure to say thank you." She didn't mention anything about it being thoughtful or too expensive to keep. I think all those years being a preacher's wife made Mama an expert at accepting charity.

"Well, Miss Amelia," Margo LaRue said as she was pinning a towel around my neck. "Do you have anything special in mind?"

There was no way I was going to tell her I wanted to look like Audrey Hepburn, so I just said, "I like those short cuts I've seen in magazines—the ones with the shaggy backs and uneven bangs."

Fancy was getting a pitcher of lemonade out of the

refrigerator. "Like Audrey Hepburn," she said. "Amelia's absolutely crazy about that woman."

"I am not!" I said, embarrassed.

Fancy walked over to Margo LaRue and said, all know-it-all, "No, really, I'm serious. She even wrote to Hollywood to get an autographed picture. It's hanging over her bed right now. She told me so."

"It is not!" I lied.

"That's what you said—that it's right next to Bobby Darin." She looked back at Margo LaRue. "She brought them over and showed them to me when they came in the mail." She looked at me, annoyed. "That's when you told me you were going to put them over your bed. Why are you lying about it?"

"I'm *not* lying! Besides, you're in love with Ricky Nelson."

"I am not! I just like the way he sings."

"Give me a *break*," I said. "You talk about how cute he is all the time."

"Oh, who cares," she muttered, then turned away.

"Okay, let's get started," Margo LaRue said. "And I agree with you, Amelia. I think Audrey Hepburn is the most beautiful woman I've ever seen." She chuckled. "Bobby Darin's not bad either." Then she looked at Fancy. "And Ricky Nelson would make anybody melt." She picked up chunks of my hair, anchored them in place with metal clips, and started cutting.

Fancy brought three glasses of lemonade over to the table. She sat across from me, regular-faced, while I glared at her. But then I started concentrating on the long strands of hair that were falling onto the newspapers Margo LaRue had spread under the chair and I wondered if there'd be any hair left on my head.

"*Wow!* Does that ever look nice," Fancy said when my haircut was finished. "And you look *just* like Audrey Hepburn—only without the dark eyes." She tilted her head, examined me good, then "Hm-m-m" floated from her mouth, slow and lazy. "Your nose and mouth are different and your neck's not as long, but other than that, you two could be twins!"

I tried not to laugh, but I couldn't help it. Fancy is one girl you cannot stay mad at for long.

"Go see what you think," Margo LaRue said, all twittery. She handed me my glasses.

Fancy followed me into the bathroom and stood next to me as I looked in the mirror. "Well?" she asked.

I smiled, but then because my hair looked so good, all I could concentrate on was my broken tooth and Mama's ugly glasses. "It looks nice," I said, lame.

Fancy's eyebrows shot up. "*Nice?* It looks *great*! What's wrong with you?"

"Nothing's wrong with me. I *told* you I like it." A darkness crept into my brain and I felt stupid thinking a new haircut would work magic. As long as I had my long hair, I could hide behind it and stay pretty much invisible. But that cute haircut had pulled back the curtain and now I was out in the open, feeling like a freak. "I have to go home now," I said. "I don't feel very well."

"What's wrong?" Fancy asked. "You felt fine a minute ago."

"I don't know," I said. "My stomach hurts."

"Amelia's got a stomachache," Fancy told Margo LaRue when we returned to the kitchen. "She's going home."

"Oh, that's too bad, sweetie. Just a second, I'll give you a ride."

I was about to say that I didn't need one, but then I thought, *There's nobody I'd rather be with right now.* "Okay," I said. "Thanks."

"What's the matter, Amelia?" Margo LaRue asked when we were sitting in her car. "Don't you like your new haircut?"

"It's not that," I said. "My hair looks great." Tears burned my eyes. "It's just that the rest of me is such a mess."

She fished a Kleenex out of her pocket, then dabbed at my cheeks. "The rest of you is gorgeous," she said. "You just need a little help around the edges—some new glasses, a trip to the dentist, and some cute clothes would do the trick."

I felt embarrassed that she'd noticed my shortcomings. Worse, she might as well have said I needed a Rolls-Royce. "My mother would never pay for any of that," I said, crying even harder.

"Well, maybe *she* wouldn't, but *you* could."

I had exactly fifty-seven cents in the jar I kept on my closet shelf behind my extra blanket. I could stop going to the movies and save my trash cash, but that would never be enough. "I don't have any money," I said, a little bit angry. I couldn't imagine her teasing me about something so important, but that's what it seemed like.

"I guess you'll just have to make some," she said. Her eyes were serious.

"How? Who's going to hire a kid?"

She shrugged. But she had an open look on her face that gave me the courage to say, "Would you?"

"Sure."

"To do what?" Maybe she wanted me to clean her apartment—and her car, but that would never be enough.

"Look," she said. "I have a little money saved and I'll lend you enough to get what you need. Then you can pay me back by helping me."

"Helping you do what?" The first thing that came to mind was her job at the funeral home. I wanted those things so bad, I'd even go there. Then I remembered her tiny apartment. "I can't take your money," I said. "It's for your new house."

"I've waited this long," she said. "A little longer isn't going to kill me. Besides, you won't be taking it, you'll be earning it. And with your help, I'll be able to save money a lot faster, so it'll work out for both of us."

"Really?"

"Absolutely."

"But what could *I* do?"

"Well, you could help me at Shady Oaks. The combs and clippers and scissors have to be disinfected after each person. You could take out rollers, hand me permanent papers, do brush outs, lots of things." Her face lit up. "And most of the people are lonely and need attention. You could visit with them while I work. Half of my time is spent listening to their memories. And as much as I enjoy that, it sure does slow me down."

"I could do that," I said.

"Of course you could. And I'd love it if you'd help me deliver my Avon orders and hand out the new catalogs."

A shiver of excitement ran through me. "When would you want me to work?"

"Maybe Saturday mornings at Shady Oaks, and when you have time, you can help me out with the Avon orders. How does that sound?"

"Fine, but I could work more than that at Shady Oaks."

"We'll see," she said. She looked at me, no-

nonsense. "But before we do anything, you have to okay this with your mother, and I don't know how that's going to turn out. I just don't want to give her any more grief than I already have."

Well, there it was. I knew there had to be a catch.

When Mama got home, I had supper ready: baked pork chops, boiled potatoes, and creamed carrots—all cooked the way I'd seen her do it forever—and applesauce from a jar to sweeten her up.

I watched for her out the kitchen window, and when she was almost at the door, I opened it. "Hi, Mama," I said. "I hope you're hungry. Supper's all ready."

"What happened to your hair?" she asked, then walked past me like her feet hurt.

"I got it cut. Do you like it?"

"I'll be right back. I need to freshen up."

While she was gone, I set the table, laid the food out, and practiced my story again in my head.

"Sit down, Mama," I said when she came back. "You look tired." I could smell the rose-scented soap she'd used to wash up—the soap that reminded her of her own mother. She had to buy it special at the drugstore. It was the one luxury she allowed herself.

"I *am* tired," she groaned. "Please pass the pork chops."

When her plate was all filled up good and she had started to eat, I said, "How was work?"

She stopped chewing and looked at me, puzzled. "What do you mean?"

Usually we just ate—no small talk. But I knew after supper wouldn't be any good. Lately she'd been falling asleep in front of the TV or going directly to bed, so I had to get it out while she was still awake.

"I was wondering if anything exciting happened."

"Nothing happened at work—just work." She took another bite of pork chop, small because she had bad teeth. Going to the dentist would never have occurred to her. She was as stingy with herself as she was with me.

While she finished eating, I tried to picture the young girl behind the luncheonette counter in Woolworth's all those years ago. And I wondered what she'd be like now if my father had stayed on the farm and she'd married somebody else—somebody who hadn't chosen her because she owned a house and could play the piano, somebody who would have loved her and been true.

"You work hard, Mama," I said. I picked at a hangnail so I didn't have to look directly at her.

"Um-hum," she said around the mouthful of potatoes she was working on. "Always have."

Low, rambling notes of the country music Mama

loved came from the radio by the sink and interfered with my thoughts. I could feel my courage melting away, so I took a deep breath and then jumped in headfirst. "A woman offered me a job today."

That got her attention and she looked up. "What woman?"

"She's Mrs. Nelson's friend—the one who cut my hair."

"Is she a colored woman? You're not working for any coloreds." The words rolled out of her mouth, matter-of-fact.

I shook my head. "She's not colored." Actually, that was pretty much a fib. All the makeup Margo LaRue wore made her a lot more colored than most people.

"What does she want you to do?" She stared at me, didn't blink.

"Oh, just wash combs and clippers, take out rollers, tidy up, stuff like that." I didn't mention the Avon deliveries. Maybe Margo LaRue was the only Avon Lady in Sullivan's Falls, and that could turn on me real quick.

"Does she have her own shop?" Mama reached for the applesauce.

"No. She goes to people's houses. I guess it's kind of a part-time job."

Mama closed her eyes and rubbed the heel of her hand over her forehead as if she had a headache.

"What's this woman's name?" she asked. Her voice sounded suspicious.

I only knew the wrong answer, so I lied. "I'm not sure," I said. "I think Mrs. Nelson called her Mary Roe," which was kind of what Margo sounded like when it came out of Mrs. Nelson's mouth.

Mama leaned forward and wiped small pearls of moisture from her upper lip. "What would you do with the money?"

Outside, a dog barked, low and mean—probably the German shepherd from down the street that I was so afraid of.

"Well, I need new glasses," I said, pointing to the adhesive tape on the broken piece. I'd colored it brown with shoe polish to match the rest of the frame, but it stuck out round like one of Mama's bunions. "And I'd like to get my tooth fixed." I smiled wide so she could see. "It looks pretty bad." I didn't mention new clothes because there were still a bunch in the attic that Mama thought were good enough. "Plus, I'll be able to buy my own school supplies, so you won't have to."

I waited while she finished the last of her coffee.

"All right," she said finally. "I don't see any harm in it. You're old enough. Just make sure you're home in time to make supper." She pushed her plate away, then gave it a little pat. "That tasted good—real good."

Something inside of me came alive—as if I'd just turned a corner in my life and was finally headed in the right direction.

As Mama walked toward the living room, she turned and looked back at me. "Your hair looks nice," she said. "They delivered the new magazines down at the store today. There's one with Audrey Hepburn on the cover. You look just like her."

17

Rice pudding, rugelach, and Newport menthols

Here's number sixteen," Fancy said. We were on Braman Street, delivering Margo LaRue's Avon orders. We parked our bikes by the porch and headed up the steps of a little white bungalow with a Welcome sign near the door—one of those irregular-shaped signs with red hearts and yellow flowers and blue doves painted along the border, all friendly and inviting. This was my first customer, so having Fancy there gave me the nerve to ring the bell.

"Miss Thatcher?" I asked when a slim, middle-aged woman with a dreamy look and a pageboy haircut answered the door.

"Yes?" At first, her face matched that welcome sign, but when her eyes had time to adjust to the midafternoon sun and she could see us good, her expression changed to cautious. "What is it you girls want?" she asked. Her tone was all business, and I could tell she was ready to close the door fast if we made a move in her direction.

I just stood there, and when Fancy realized I was hopeless, she grabbed the bag I was holding and showed it to Miss Thatcher. "We're here to deliver your Avon order for Miss LaRue." Charm oozed out of her like honey from one of those plastic squeeze bears.

I hadn't been to the dentist or the eye doctor yet, and I was still wearing my sisters' old clothes, so I was a disaster. But Fancy was decked out fine in one of her expensive summer outfits, and she was wearing the solid gold charm bracelet the judge gave her for her birthday. It took a second for Miss Thatcher's brain to wake up, but when it did, she stammered, "Are you Judge Watson's—um . . . his . . . ah . . ."

"I'm his granddaughter, ma'am," Fancy said.

"Well, yes. That's what I meant," Miss Thatcher agreed. She fiddled with the half-glasses that hung on a chain around her neck and said, "So you're the Frances I've heard so much about."

"Fancy, ma'am."

"Pardon me?"

"I like to be called Fancy. It's my nickname."

"Oh, well, of course," Miss Thatcher said, all interested. "Fancy."

Fancy was being treated better since the secret was out. Nobody was falling over themselves to impress her, but the fact that she was Judge Watson's granddaughter seemed to have won her brownie points, especially with people like Miss Thatcher.

Miss Thatcher examined me with a you-remind-me-of-somebody look, and I wondered if she had known my father. Finally she said, "You must be Fancy's friend."

"Yes, I am," I said, polite. "I'm Amelia."

She didn't ask me my last name, just said, "Well, come right on in and make yourselves comfortable. I'll get you girls a cool treat," which sounded just fine to me because it was steaming hot out. Ice cream or a Coke would really hit the spot. On her way to the kitchen, she stopped and looked back. "I hope you brought a fall catalog."

"Oh, we did, ma'am," Fancy said. "And it's got all kinds of new stuff, plus a bunch of end-of-the-summer specials."

I swear that girl is going to own her own company someday—maybe even Avon. While we were riding our bikes over to Braman Street, she memorized the entire catalog. It amazed me that Fancy could ride her bike no-hands and read at the same time.

While Miss Thatcher was in the kitchen, Fancy and I waited on the couch in the living room with the

Avon bag between us. Fancy elbowed me in the ribs, then pointed to an almost-full pack of Newport menthols on the coffee table.

I gave her a blank look and mouthed, *"What?"*

"Let's take some," she whispered.

I shook my head and quickly glanced at the door to the kitchen.

By the time I looked back, Fancy was sliding two cigarettes out of the package. Then she lifted her shirt, anchored them under the waistband of her shorts, and pulled her top back down.

"Well, here you go, ladies," Miss Thatcher said as she came back into the room, carrying two big bowls. "I hope you like rice pudding."

Rice pudding! I thought. I *hate* rice pudding, especially if it has raisins in it.

"I added lots of raisins," Miss Thatcher said, proud. "I've heard how much kids like them."

I think it should be against the law for people to spring weird food on you anytime they feel like it—especially things like rice pudding or egg custard, slimy stuff with no taste.

"It looks delicious," Fancy said after Miss Thatcher handed her a dish. "I love rice pudding!"

"Thanks," I said when I got mine. "It does look good." I patted my stomach and sighed. "But I don't think I'll be able to finish all this. I just had lunch."

Miss Thatcher looked at her watch. "But it's three o'clock."

Fancy held up the Avon bag. "Here's your order," she said fast, rescuing me from my lie. "Miss LaRue put your bill inside."

"Her phone number's on it," I added. "She said to tell you that she'll be by soon to demonstrate the new products, but if you need anything before she comes, just give her a call."

"That's fine," Miss Thatcher said as she took the bag. "I'll get my checkbook. It's in the bedroom."

As soon as she was gone, I turned to Fancy, pointed at my dish, and made a *yuck* face. "I can't eat this," I whispered. "What should I do with it?"

"Just a sec." She wolfed down the rest of her pudding then traded bowls with me.

Miss Thatcher came back, handed me the check, and when she saw the empty dishes on the coffee table, she said all bouncy, "I see the rice pudding was a hit. How about seconds?"

I stood up and shook my head. "I couldn't eat another bite, but it was delicious. Thank you."

Fancy followed my lead and said, "No more for me either, but it was really good."

Miss Thatcher's neck turned a splotchy pink. "Do you think Judge Watson would like it?" she asked. "I can write out the recipe in a jiffy."

"That would be nice," Fancy said. "But—um . . . uh . . . he's allergic to rice."

Miss Thatcher cocked her head to one side. "I've never heard of anybody being allergic to rice."

"Or maybe it's raisins," Fancy said. "I know it's one or the other."

"Well, then," Miss Thatcher said, opening the front door. "Give him my best." She hesitated, then added, "And say hello to your mother for me. Maybe we could get together for coffee someday. You tell her that, okay?"

"I surely will," Fancy said as we stepped out onto the porch. And on her way down the steps, she mumbled, "Yeah, *right*. Like I'm really gonna do that."

"Bye, girls," Miss Thatcher said. "I'll be sure to make rice pudding the next time you come." She looked at me and said, "You know, Amelia, I never did get your last name."

"That's okay," I said, as if I hadn't heard her right. "See you later."

"But—oh—well, no matter."

As soon as the door closed, Fancy said, cross, "I hope you never expect me to go through that again. Before that snivel-nosed biddy knew who my grandfather was, she wouldn't have let my mother shine her shoes. Now she wants to be her friend? And that was the worst rice pudding I've ever tasted. I think she made it with sour milk and rotten eggs." She grabbed her bike and smacked up the kickstand. "And those raisins were so hard I had to swallow them whole."

I reached for my bike. "Well, then, why did you eat mine, too?"

She shot me a look that would have cracked a rock. "So we could get out of there. When I saw you stirring yours around and around—staring at it like it was poison—I figured we'd be stuck on that couch for hours."

"We would have," I said. "There was no way I could eat that stuff."

She pulled up her shirt and pointed to the cigarettes. "At least we got these."

I started pedaling next to her. "Why do you want those things anyway?"

"Because I've never tried one before. Have you?"

"No."

"Don't you want to?"

I pictured Audrey Hepburn in *Breakfast at Tiffany's*. "Yeah, I guess."

Fancy pointed to the Avon bag in my bike basket. "Let's deliver that and get home. We need matches."

"Okay," I said. "Miss Weinman lives at the end of the street. Margo LaRue said she's really nice."

"Well, I don't care how nice she is," Fancy said. "I'm not going to be suckered into eating anything."

"Me neither." I laughed. "We'll give her the bag, get the money, and leave."

Miss Weinman was asleep on a rusty front porch swing. A huge yellow cat was curled up beside her with its paw on her cheek. Another cat, a small tortoiseshell, sat on a wooden table, lapping up what was left of a mug of coffee, which must have been there awhile because a milk skin floated on the top and pieces of it hung from the cat's chin in long, soft strings.

Miss Weinman had tan, leathery skin and salt-and-pepper hair. She was dressed in denim coveralls like farmers wear over a plain white T-shirt, topped with a worn cardigan sweater, no jewelry.

Fancy and I stood there not knowing what to do until finally the tortoiseshell cat jumped from the table and landed on Miss Weinman's stomach. "Oomph" came out of her mouth, and when she saw us staring at her, she sat up fast. At first, there was fear in her eyes, but then her shoulders relaxed and she said, "I hope I wasn't snoring." She wiped the corners of her mouth. "Or drooling." She laughed. "I seem to do both when I really get into a good nap."

"You weren't," I said. There was something about Miss Weinman that made me feel calm. "We're here to deliver your Avon order."

"Well, then, you must be Amelia Rye," Miss Weinman said. When she smiled, her dark eyes turned playful. "Margo's told me a lot of nice things about you."

My face turned hot—from the compliment, but also because she might know my mother and mention that I was working for Margo LaRue.

I pointed to Fancy to get the attention away from me. "And this is my friend, Fancy Nelson."

"Hello, Fancy," Miss Weinman said. "It's nice to meet you. Margo mentioned you might be coming, that you two are inseparable." And she left it at that. No fawning over Fancy because of her grandfather.

Miss Weinman wiped sweat from her forehead with the palm of her hand. "I didn't realize how hot it was," she said. She got up from the swing and motioned to it. "Sit down, girls. I'll get you something to eat."

"Oh, that's okay," Fancy said. "We're not hungry."

"I am," I said. "I'd love something to eat."

Miss Weinman headed for the door with the yellow cat right behind her.

"What's the matter with you?" Fancy whispered when we were alone. "I thought we were going to get out of here."

"I just want to stay a little longer," I said. "Margo LaRue was right. Miss Weinman *is* nice."

"What's so special about *her*?" Fancy asked.

"I don't know," I said. And I didn't. "I just like her is all."

Fancy shook her head and looked pained. "You sure are weird sometimes." She took in a huge breath and let it out—loud. "I'm going home," she said, annoyed.

"I'd rather do nothing than eat prunes or whatever antique food she's going to bring out." As she was riding away, she called back, "When you're done here, stop at my house." She patted her shirt where she'd hidden the cigarettes. "We still have to try these out."

While I was waiting for Miss Weinman to come back, I sat on the swing and looked at the tottering pile of books on the floor next to it. They were the thick, hardcover kind with difficult titles, not like the dime-store romance stories Mama read.

I was watching a spider build a web in an elbow of the porch railing and thinking how amazing that was when the tortoiseshell cat jumped on my lap and started washing the milk off her face. When she got good and settled in, her motor turned on, and her purr sounded as if she had a sore throat—low and raspy with a squeaky little *yip* thrown in now and then.

"Where's Fancy?" Miss Weinman said as she was backing out the screen door. She'd taken off the sweater, and her arms looked old and wrinkled like Mama's. What caught my eye more than anything, though, was the mean row of blue-black numbers tattooed just below the crease of her elbow. At the time, I suspected those numbers meant that she'd been through something evil. I just didn't know then how truly evil it was.

"Fancy had to go home and clean her room," I said.

"She asked me to say bye and that she was glad to meet you." The fact that I could lie so easily was starting to worry me.

"I see you've made another friend," Miss Weinman said as she set a plate of something delicious-looking on the wooden table—golden brown, twisty things. "Abby doesn't cozy up to many people."

"She's really sweet," I said. "I love cats."

"She can tell that you do." Miss Weinman reached over and tickled the cat's ear. "I'll be right back. I have to get the drinks."

Abby'd finished her bath, and she started licking my fingers with her sandpaper tongue, then turned up the volume on her purr. I wished so much that Mama would let me have a cat. But no. She'd had her fill of them when she was raising her other kids.

Miss Weinman came back, holding two Cokes with candy-stripe straws bobbing out the tops. "Here you go," she said, handing me one. Then she reached for the plate of goodies and held it in front of me. "I made these this morning. Have you had rugelach before?"

At first, I was going to say, "Sure. I've had them lots of times," so I wouldn't sound ignorant. But there was something in Miss Weinman's face that told me I didn't have to impress her, that I could just be my own plain self. So I said, "No, I've never even heard of them."

After I'd helped myself, she took one, put the plate

back on the table, and sat next to me on the swing. "They're Jewish, like me," she said with a smile in her voice. "When I was a little girl, my mother taught me how to make them—the way her mother had taught her." A cloud rolled over her face for just a second as she looked down at the numbers on her arm. But then she came back from wherever she'd gone. "These are raspberry. The recipe calls for raisins, but I just can't stomach those things, so I leave them out."

Being Jewish was a sin in Mama's book, almost as bad as being colored. And I'd heard her hateful comments for as long as I could remember. But when I looked over at Miss Weinman's easy face with her mouth full of the most delicious treat I'd ever tasted, I felt kind of sorry for Mama because she kept herself locked in such a small, sad world.

"I don't like raisins either," I said. "So I'm glad you left them out."

She laughed and reached for the plate. "Have another one."

"Thanks," I said. "These are good."

While we finished eating, we didn't say anything, just sat there and enjoyed the food and the day. Funny how sometimes, when you are comfortable with a person, no words are needed.

Abby'd gone back to polishing her fur, and when she was satisfied that it was perfect, she stood up, stretched, then jumped down to find another place to be. She'd been lying on the Avon bag, and when I saw it, I remembered why I was there. I straightened it out as much as I could and handed it to Miss Weinman. "This is your order," I said, apologetic. "Margo LaRue said the slip is inside."

Miss Weinman grinned, then held out the bag and blew off a huge tuft of cat hair. "I can't even remember what I ordered," she said as she opened the bag. "Most of the time, I buy things just to help Margo. She's had a hard life. Her parents died when she was young and she has no other family to speak of. She's a woman on her own, like me." Miss Weinman took out a pink perfume box with a bouquet of lilacs painted on the front. "Oh, that's right. I have a friend who just loves the scent of lilacs." She put the box on her lap, looked over at me, and her voice turned serious. "I'm glad that you and Margo get along so well," she said. "You're like the daughter she's always wished for." She smiled, soft. "You fill the hole she's had in her heart for so long."

I thought about what Miss Weinman said, that Margo LaRue didn't have a mother or a father she could love. Then I thought how much older my daddy was and how, at first, he treated her as if she was perfect. "Maybe that's why she loved *my* father," I said.

Miss Weinman turned to me and, with a satisfied

sigh, said, "You're a very intelligent girl, Amelia. I can see why Margo thinks you're so special."

"Hold still," Fancy said. "We're almost out of matches."

"I *am* holding still," I said. "I can't help it that the wind keeps blowing them out." We were standing next to Judge Watson's garage, and Fancy was trying to light my cigarette.

"There, it's lit," she said. "Now I'll do mine."

"Well, hurry up," I said. "I need to make supper before my mother gets home."

Fancy took a tiny puff of her cigarette and blew out a thin stream of smoke. "I bet old Miss Whatever-her-name-is made you eat Cream of Wheat and then listen to boring stories about when she was our age. You should have left when I did. You could have come here and had a Coke."

"I *did have* a Coke," I said. I took a long drag on my cigarette and breathed it in deep—like I'd seen Grandpa Thomas do—then blew the smoke out my nose.

"Hey, you're really good," Fancy said. "How'd you learn to do that?"

"It's easy," I said, and then coughed. "Just put the cigarette in your mouth and take in a big breath—like this."

She did. Then her face turned white, really white.

And before I could say anything, she threw up—huge. Seeing her mess made my own stomach switch gears, and in one quick second, my rugelach had joined her rice pudding and raisins.

"Oh my God," Fancy groaned. "I've never felt so sick in my whole life."

"Me neither," I said. "I have to lie down."

"I do, too," Fancy said.

We smashed out our cigarettes in the dirt, then walked over to the apple tree by the garage, curled up under it, held our stomachs, and moaned.

We both heard a car door close, but neither of us moved. I was hoping it was somebody with a gun who liked to kill young girls. Instead, there was laughing— loud, deep belly laughing—and then Judge Watson's voice. "You girls don't look so good," he said, still chuckling. "Would you like a cigarette? It might make you feel better."

"Noooooooooooooo" came out of both of us at the same time.

"You sure? I could go get you some. I see you still have some matches left."

"Noooooooooooooo."

Judge Watson knelt down and patted our shoulders. "There are some lessons in life you just have to learn the painful way." He wasn't laughing anymore, and his voice was kind. "I'll be right back," he said. "I'll bring something that will make you feel better."

After we'd taken the Pepto-Bismol, Judge Watson helped us to the house and up to Fancy's room. As we went through the kitchen, Mrs. Nelson put her hands on her hips and said, "Your grandfather told me you got into the green apples. I told you those weren't for eating, that they'd give you a bellyache. I guess you won't do that again."

I shook my head, and Fancy said, "Nope. No more green apples."

As Judge Watson was leaving Fancy's room, he winked at us and said, "Next time you're on your own."

When I felt a little better, I rode my bike home and got into bed. I didn't even care that Mama yelled at me for not having supper ready.

18

Peacocks, chic outfits, and traitors

On the first day of sixth grade, there I was with my Audrey Hepburn haircut, cat's-eye glasses with thin plastic lenses and blue frames to match my eyes, a perfect front tooth, and my beautiful new skirt and sweater outfit. I finally knew how the popular girls must feel.

It didn't take long for me to realize that even though I was gussied up like a peacock, in the other kids' eyes, I was still the drab sparrow I'd always been. My new look didn't erase the fact that I was the girl who lived in the dilapidated house at the edge of town with her mean old mother who worked at the grocery store and yelled at kids for sampling the grapes. It didn't change who my father was or that my grandfather used to drink too much and make a spectacle of himself.

Our teacher, Miss Annie Pine, told me I looked pretty, though. She'd been around as long as Miss Dumfrey and knew everything about everybody, too, only she was nice, one of those adults that kids respect because she does the same for them.

"Welcome, Amelia," she said. "That's your seat in the second row." I thought it was so considerate of her to put me right next to Fancy. That's the kind of thing that makes her so special—the kind of thing most teachers wouldn't even think of doing.

Miss Pine didn't give us homework on the first day, so after school, Margo LaRue took me clothes shopping. Fancy came along because she didn't have anything else to do. Plus, she thinks she's an expert in the fashion department, which she pretty much is. I sure had no idea what I was doing, and as much as I like Margo LaRue, hers wasn't the look I was going for.

Margo LaRue pointed to a mannequin in the middle of the floor. "How about this outfit? I think it would look good on you."

"That's a great look," Fancy said. "Kilts are really popular this year. And I love the blouse and the kneesocks. The whole thing is very chic."

We were in Markson's Department Store, right across the street from the A&P. Mama wouldn't see me, though, because the front window of the grocery store was plastered with giant-size sales flyers. Plus, the meat department was way in the back.

When we left the store, I had my very chic outfit in a very chic Markson's bag. While Fancy and Margo LaRue were talking about clothes, I glanced over at the A&P. The front door was open, and Mama was standing there, watching us. Someone she worked with must have seen me and tattled. Part of me felt guilty. But there was another part of me that was glad. That part wanted to hold up the package and say, mean, "This was your job. You're supposed to take me shopping. You're supposed to care." I expected her to throw a fit, but she didn't say anything, just lowered her head, turned, and disappeared into the shadows. Then the part of me that was glad disappeared, too.

At supper, Mama and I ate in silence. When she was finished, she took off her glasses and massaged the red pressure spots on her nose. Those glasses were the same faded plastic ones she'd worn for as long as I could remember. Finally, she put them back on and looked over at me. I thought she was going to lay into me about being a traitor, but she just stared at me and my beautiful new glasses. As I looked at her tired eyes, I wished she *had* yelled at me. Not saying anything meant that I was worse than a traitor. It meant that I wasn't even worth the breath it would take to tell me so.

19

Dancing to Bobby Darin

It's funny how sometimes you just know a thing. It was Saturday morning, early December, and I was walking home from helping Margo LaRue at Shady Oaks when I saw him sitting on our front porch steps with a folded-over paper bag next to him. He was skinny like me with long arms and legs, my color hair. His clothes didn't fit. He had on baggy brown pants, a denim jacket with too-short sleeves, black dress shoes—the kind old men wear—and white gym socks. And when I got closer, I wasn't surprised to see his china blue eyes.

He stood up and put his hand in his pants pocket. "Hi," he said, quiet. "I'm waiting for Mr. and Mrs. Rye, but I guess they don't live here anymore." He grabbed the bag and started to walk away.

"Jack?" The word slid from my mouth so easily you'd think I'd said it to him a million times.

He looked back at me, jingled change in his pocket, and narrowed his eyes. "Yeah?" Then he glanced over his shoulder as if there might be someone sneaking up on him.

"I'm Amelia. Your sister," I said.

His shoulders relaxed and he took his hand out of his pocket. "My *sister*?" A tiny smile started, and then it grew huge. "She had another kid?"

"Yup," I said. "Me."

He raised his arms toward the cold gray sky, turned clear around on his heel, and laughed. "Wow! That must have been a shock."

"She sure didn't do it on purpose," I said. "Mama nearly killed Daddy when she found out I was on the way."

"I'm not surprised. He wasn't exactly the family-man type."

"What do you mean? Didn't he like kids?"

He started to say something, but stopped and looked at me for a long minute. "It's not that. It's just that he wasn't home a lot, being a preacher and all." The dark look on Jack's face didn't match his words, and I wondered if he was hiding something. But then his expression changed to pleasant and he stopped to calculate something in his head. "Ma had to be pushing fifty," he said with amazement in his voice.

"I know." I'd never said anything to anybody, not even Fancy, but the fact that Mama was old enough to be my grandmother was embarrassing.

"So how long ago *was* that?" he asked. "I mean, how old are you?"

"Eleven."

He looked at me, kind of sad. "You seem older."

That wasn't the first time I'd heard that. I think when kids don't have parents who care for them, they grow up fast.

I was wearing a new winter coat—navy blue wool with gold buttons—that I bought with my Avon money. Jack touched my shoulder, light. "Well, at least they take good care of you. You look like a million bucks."

"Thanks," I said. "But they don't—"

"I guess you know where I've been," he said fast, as if he needed to get it out and over with.

I nodded.

He looked straight into my eyes. "Are you okay with it?"

"I'm okay." I'd always been okay with it. Driving a getaway car had never seemed like a very big deal to me.

He let out a heavy breath that looked like smoke when it hit the cold air.

"Anyway, how come you were sent to prison for just driving a car?" I asked. "I mean, it wasn't like you were going to hurt anybody."

"It's the law. I was just as guilty as if I'd gone into that gas station and robbed those people." He shrugged. "It's just the way it is."

Well, I didn't think that was fair, but I suppose the people who got robbed did. There was an awkward silence. I guess Jack was giving me a chance to ask him more about prison, but I didn't. I was fine with letting that go forever.

"So where are they?" Jack asked, glancing over at the house. "I rang the bell and knocked, but nobody answered. Ma never used to go anywhere."

I thought how much things had changed since Jack lived at home, and it amazed me that nobody had gone to see him in all those years. Plus, if Mama'd treated him like a regular kid, he wouldn't have ended up in prison. After I filled him in on what had happened while he was gone, he sighed and then said, "It must have hit Ma pretty hard when Dad left."

"I guess," I said. "But she drove him away with her meanness."

"I wouldn't call her mean," he said. "I don't think her life turned out the way she hoped it would. I just remember her cleaning and cooking and trying to raise three kids on hardly any money. I think she did the best she could." Then he laughed a little. "And the only thing she could control was the way her kids behaved—so she worked pretty hard doing that."

I nodded. "She still does."

Jack smiled.

Then I said, "Grandpa Thomas told me you left because Mama made you dress up all the time and the other kids teased you and called you a sissy."

"That's true," he agreed.

"Is that why you ran away?" I asked. "Because those kids made fun of you?" I couldn't imagine anybody making fun of him. He was tall and good-looking and he smelled like hard work and big muscles.

"It wasn't them," he said. "They were just being kids."

It must have been Sylvia, I thought. She'd make anybody want to get away. But she would have been grown and gone by then. "Was it Charlotte?"

"No. Poor little Charlotte was already in the asylum."

"Well, then, *who*?" There wasn't anybody left.

"It was Grandpa Thomas," Jack said, low.

"Grandpa Thomas?" That couldn't possibly be true. And hearing Jack lie like that made me back away from him. "Grandpa Thomas wouldn't hurt anybody," I said.

Jack shook his head. "Not when he was sober."

I pulled my fists into my sleeves and set my jaw tight. "What are you talking about?" I knew what Jack meant, but I couldn't stand to hear anybody talk bad about Grandpa Thomas.

"Look," he said. "I was young then and I was already an outcast. He couldn't help what he did when he was drunk, but I thought the least he could do was to stay at the farm and do his drinking there instead of coming to Sullivan's Falls and making an ass of himself out in public in front of the kids I had to go to school with." Jack buried the toe of his shoe under a layer of dead leaves on the lawn. "But I should have stood up to the morons who jerked me around. If I'd known then what I know now, I would have ignored them." He gave me a straight-line smile. "And leaving was a mistake. I should have stayed here and finished school and none of that other crap would have happened. It's not his fault. It's mine."

I relaxed a little, but didn't say anything.

Then his look turned somber. "The worst thing was the shitty letter I sent him before I left." He looked over at the house. "Sorry. I know I'm not supposed to curse around here."

"What letter?"

"I told him I hated him for ruining my life and that I never wanted to see him again." Tears filled his eyes and he quickly wiped them away. "Then I up and disgraced *him* even more than he did me."

The wind blew colder, and Jack started rubbing his hands together.

"Do you want to go inside?" I asked. "I can make us something to eat."

"That'd be great," he said. "I'm starving, but how about if I make *you* lunch?"

A vision of bread and water came into my head, but I said, "Sure. I'd like that."

I handed him the key. When we walked into the living room, he just stood there and looked around. "It's exactly the same," he said, with surprise in his voice. "Except there's a TV where the record player used to be. I wonder where it is now."

"It's in Grandpa Thomas's room at the end of the hall," I said.

"Is it okay if I take a look?" he asked, like I was the boss of the house. "I'd like to see my old records."

I shrugged. "Sure."

As Jack started toward the bedrooms, he tapped the corner of an end table and said, "My photo used to be right there." He looked back at me and chuckled. "In my Sunday best, of course."

Mama must have thrown that photo out, because I'd snooped through every inch of the house and I never saw it.

"This used to be mine," Jack said as we went into Grandpa Thomas's bedroom. He looked through the drawers and in the closet, even under the bed. "There's nothing left," he said. "Not even my baseball cards." His voice sounded empty. "It's as if I never existed."

I walked over to the corner. "Here's the record player," I said, trying to make him feel better.

He ran his hand over the polished wood, then opened the top. "I remember when we were small and Charlotte was still okay, she used to sing along to the records. She had such a sweet little voice."

It surprised me that, even though she was two years older, Jack talked as if Charlotte was younger than him. "What happened to her?" I asked. "Mama never mentioned anything about it."

"I don't know what it's called," he said. "But when she was sixteen, she started to disappear from life. Finally she just curled up in the corner of the room, rocked back and forth, and hummed—just one note in that sweet voice of hers. If anybody got near her, she'd kick and scream as if they were trying to kill her. Then she started hearing voices."

I couldn't even imagine how terrible that must have been. "Did anybody try to help her?"

"*Everybody* did. But then she started hurting herself." He lowered his eyes. "That's when they took her to the asylum—so she could be with doctors who treat that kind of thing."

I nodded, didn't say anything.

I think Jack wanted to lighten the mood, so he

pulled some records out of the cabinet and said, "Let's see if this thing still works."

"It works," I said. "Grandpa Thomas and I used to listen to it all the time."

"What's your favorite song?" he asked.

"Uh—I like 'Dream Lover.' But it's not there. That's just dusty old stuff."

"Ah, so you're a Bobby Darin fan," he said, in kind of a teasing way.

I felt my face turn hot. "He's a good singer," I said, looking at my feet.

He gave me a soft jab in the arm with his elbow. "Not bad-looking either, right?"

"He's okay," I said, grinning like a goof.

Jack started sorting through the records and said, "I'm going to show you what *real* music sounds like."

I wrinkled my nose. "Those things are ancient."

"Yeah," he said, smiling. "Tunes for dinosaurs."

When he'd finished searching, he said, "Mine aren't here anymore." He put the records back. "Let's go eat. I'm really hungry."

"Me, too," I said.

I started for the kitchen, but Jack headed toward the front door.

"Come on," he said. "I'll treat. Is Barney's Diner still in business?"

"Yeah," I said, but I wondered how he could afford to buy lunch. "I could make sandwiches and we can eat them here at home," I offered, afraid to hurt his feelings.

Jack realized what I was up to and said, "Don't worry. I have money."

When I looked surprised, he laughed. "I had a job in the kitchen that paid two dollars a week. If you're not a smoker, you can save quite a bit—at least enough to buy your baby sister lunch."

I smiled—big.

"Plus, I learned how to cook," he said. He made believe he was flipping a pancake with a spatula. Then he pretended to toss it into the air, and we waited and waited and waited, but it never did come back down.

As I walked next to my funny brother, I felt safe for the first time since Grandpa Thomas had gone away. At Barney's, Elvis Presley was belting out "Return to Sender" on the jukebox. Jack chose a booth by the window.

"How are you two today?" the waitress asked in a sunny voice as she filled our water glasses.

"Well, I can't speak for the young lady," Jack said. "But *I've* never been better."

"I'm fine, too," I said, thinking how much happier Jack was than when we were in Mama's house. It was as if he could finally relax and be himself.

After we gave the waitress our order, it seemed like all the words in the world had disappeared. We just sat there like two mutes. Finally, he said, "The place looks good. They've really done it up nice—even added that little dance floor by the jukebox."

"Yup, it looks a lot better," I said. I had no idea what I was talking about because I'd never been there before. The only times I went to restaurants were when Judge Watson and Mrs. Nelson took Fancy and me out to eat, and that was usually to Howard Johnson's or Dairy Queen and once to a fancy Italian place for spaghetti.

"Well, here you go," the waitress said as she put our Cokes in front of us. "I'll be right back with your meals."

Jack didn't even use his straw, just picked up his glass and chugged down the whole thing. And when the waitress brought our plates, he ordered another Coke.

"You sure are thirsty," she said. "You'd think you hadn't had one of those things in years."

Jack smiled at her. "You would think that, wouldn't you?"

After we finished our lunch, Jack handed me a dime and asked me to play something on the jukebox. As soon as I was back at the booth and "Dream Lover" started, he asked me to dance.

My chest tightened. "I don't know how," I said.

He got up. "That's okay. I'm not any good. We'll just do the best we can."

But he *was* good. He was real good. He held me the

way fathers on TV do when they dance with their daughters. And he didn't act annoyed when my feet got in the way. I laid my head on his chest and I felt loved—how I used to feel when I still had Grandpa Thomas whole.

"This is his room," I said. "Do you want me to wait outside so you two can be alone?" Jack and I were at Shady Oaks, and even though it wasn't as warm as it usually was in there, Jack was sweating bad.

"I've wanted to do this since I left home," he said. "But maybe you should come in. He's probably not going to be very happy to see me."

Grandpa Thomas was sitting in the red chair with his eyes closed. He hadn't moved his finger since the day after Easter. Turned out that was just a one-time thing. The nurse said it happens like that sometimes, as if a wire in his brain started working, but then it got disconnected again. When she told me that, I wanted to jiggle him good to get the wires back where they belonged. But I couldn't. And maybe God gave me that tiny miracle so I'd know for sure that Grandpa Thomas understood me when I talked to him. I kissed him on the cheek and held his hand. "There's somebody here to see you," I said. Then I put Grandpa Thomas's hand in Jack's.

"It's good to see you, Grandpa Thomas," Jack said. "It's been a long time."

Then a stream of tears flowed down Jack's cheeks and he didn't even try to wipe them away. "I'm sorry for the awful things I said to you. And I'm sorry for sending you that letter. I didn't mean any of it. And most of all, I'm sorry for making you ashamed of me." Jack knelt down, laid his head on Grandpa Thomas's knee, and just stayed like that—didn't say any more.

Grandpa Thomas's expression didn't change, but a single tear rolled down his cheek and landed on the back of Jack's neck. Jack looked up, hugged Grandpa Thomas, and then bawled like a baby. The sobs that came out of him were so huge it was as if they were trying to wash away all the sadness he'd ever felt. And then I started in. But my tears were the kind that come when something makes you feel happier than you ever thought you could be.

"I wish you wouldn't go," I said. Jack and I were standing outside Shady Oaks and he was getting ready to hitchhike to Albany.

"I have to," he said. "It wouldn't be fair to stay in Sullivan's Falls and embarrass Ma even more than I already have."

"But you just came," I whined.

He cupped my chin in his hand and smiled. "I'm not going very far," he said. "I'll find a job and save some money and I'll come back and visit."

"Will you write to me?" I asked.

"All the time. And when I get a phone, I'll call."

"Promise?"

He kissed me on the cheek, soft. "I promise."

I let go of his hand, and as he walked away, I watched him get smaller and smaller. Then a car stopped and he was gone.

When Mama came home from work, she asked me what I'd done that day.

"I met a new friend," I said, a little bit cocky.

She looked at me, cautious. "Is this one white?"

I nodded.

"Well, then you can bring this one home."

"I will," I said. "Someday I'll bring this one home."

20

Sometimes you just do a thing.

I'm coming!" I called from the kitchen. "It's almost ready." I was making a ham and cheese sandwich and heating up vegetable soup for Mama's lunch. She had tripped over a case of Dinty Moore beef stew at the A&P and hurt her ankle, and she couldn't walk by herself. Of course, she wouldn't go to the doctor, and she wasn't going to spend perfectly good money for crutches that she'd only use a few times. So *I* had to take care of her. The one good part was that I got to miss school. But the rest wasn't anything I would sit up nights wishing for.

"Don't forget the salt," Mama called.

I'd never forget the salt. Mama always doused everything good before she even tasted it. "I *won't*," I said, snippy.

When she was working, she was either too busy or

too tired to complain about the way I cooked. But with nothing to do, she had time to find fault with every little thing, even the way I scrambled her eggs, which was the same way she did it.

Mama was sitting on the couch, watching a soap opera, when I put the tray on her lap. She kept staring at the TV. "I'll need more mustard."

"But I put lots on already."

"I'll need more," she said as she took a sip of tea, then pulled back fast because it was too hot.

I'll need more mustard. I'll need more mustard, I sing-sang in my head on my way back to the kitchen. All I could think of was that her ankle had better heal pretty darn quick or there was going to be a murder—and it wouldn't be mine. But then I had an idea. It might help me to survive if I made a game out of the mess I was in. I'd treat Mama the way I wished she'd treat me and I'd pretend that she was grateful. Plus, maybe she'd notice and change her ways. That last part was wishful thinking, but it was worth a try.

"Here you go," I said, all sweet as I handed her the jar of French's and a knife. "Is there anything else you want?"

She shook her head no and motioned for me to get out of the way—I was blocking the TV.

In my head I told myself, *Thank you so much, honey. Everything looks delicious.* Then I went into the kitchen to eat my own lunch.

It is hard to know what to do with your eyes when you are helping your mother with her personal hygiene needs. I had never seen her naked before, so as I helped her into the bathtub, I tried to convince myself that an adult woman is just an overgrown kid with creepy accessories.

When I had her all settled in good with everything she needed and was about to escape, she held out the washcloth. "You can scrub my back before you go."

I was going to hand her the bath brush and get out of there, but then I remembered my plan.

"No problem, Mama," I said cheery. "I'd be glad to."

Nothing from her. But in my mind—*I really appreciate this, Amelia. I don't know what I'd do without you.*

As I was scrubbing her back with her rose-scented soap, I noticed how bent over she was and how her skin was almost as spotted as Grandpa Thomas's. And she was even getting a little bit bald on the very top of her head. It made me sad, and I started washing more gently, the way you would wash a tiny baby. When I finished, I handed her the washcloth so she could do the rest of her bath. As I was leaving the room, she looked at me. And I thought I saw just the tiniest bit of a smile.

After I had Mama back on the couch, I rode my bike to the drugstore. We were out of aspirin and *every four hours* was coming soon.

That night after I'd helped her into bed, I rubbed her sore ankle with Ben-Gay, and then I asked her the question I'd wanted to ask for as long as I could remember. "Did you ever love my father?"

She looked at me for a long time. She never did answer. But just as I was about to leave, a tear rolled down her cheek and then another one. And those tears—even better than words—told me how she felt about my daddy.

21

My mother's daughter

Your mother wants to take us where?" I asked Fancy on the way to school. It was the middle of June, almost the end of sixth grade, and already steaming hot. Plus, I'd woken up with menstrual cramps and Mama wouldn't let me stay home. If I ever get to talk to God in person, I'm going to ask Him what the hell He was thinking when He decided to give a twelve-year-old girl the curse!

"Camping," Fancy repeated. "She wants to take us camping in the woods at the end of your street. You know—the little state park by the lake."

"Why?" I said, snotty. Camping sounded like fun, but I was too miserable to be anything but smack-ass mean.

"What's the *matter* with you?" Fancy asked, even snottier. "What're you mad at me for?"

"I'm not mad at anybody. I just don't feel good."

I hadn't told Fancy that I'd gotten my period because I knew she hadn't. When she did, she'd tell the whole world, like it was something to be proud of, so I had to feel like a freak all by myself.

"Maybe you should go home," she said. "You don't look so good. Your face is kind of puffy and you've got a zit on your chin the size of a headlight."

"That's not a zit," I said, angry. "It's a mosquito bite." When I'd first looked in the mirror, that zit was hardly noticeable, but then I picked at it good. And Fancy was right. I could have lit up a coal mine with that thing. "Tell me more about your mother and this camping trip," I said to get the attention off my chin.

"She said we should start learning about the flora and the fauna of the Adirondacks."

"The *what*? And the *what*?" Sometimes Fancy is so annoying with her smarty-pants brain.

"The flora and the fauna—the plants and the animals."

"Well, why didn't you just say that in the first place?"

"Because that's what she called them and she thinks we should learn the proper terms."

I screwed my face up good. "Sometimes I think your mother's a little on the weird side."

She rolled her eyes. "I do, too. But wait. It gets even weirder."

"Weirder how?"

"She's going to be a science teacher at our new school next year."

"*She is?*" That was *great* news. "I didn't know your mother was a teacher." I couldn't imagine anybody I'd rather be in a classroom with.

"Yup. She taught in Alabama before I was born. But she had to pass a test to get her New York certification. And now she thinks I'm old enough for her to go back to work." Fancy stopped for a minute and looked as if she wasn't sure how she felt about the idea. Then she sighed and said, "I guess in Sullivan's Falls, the science teachers take their students on an overnight field trip in the woods and she wants to be ready."

"So we're guinea pigs then."

"Yeah. I guess you could say that. Oh, and Miss LaRue's coming with us."

I knew Fancy's mother and Margo LaRue had become good friends. I just couldn't picture either one of them sleeping in a tent or washing up in a lake. Then I thought about all the nice things Mrs. Nelson and Margo LaRue had done for me and how crabby I was being to Fancy. "Okay!" I said. "I'll go."

The day we went camping, I had even more fun than I thought I would. We spent the afternoon in the woods, looking for flora and fauna. We saw plenty of flora but not one single fauna, unless you count the sweet little white cat that kept following us. Margo LaRue and I wanted to keep it, but it jumped out of my arms and scurried off in the direction of the park attendant's house at the edge of the woods.

We went swimming in the lake and then made a fire and roasted hot dogs on sticks for supper. Plus, I finally got to eat a genuine s'more. And they are just as good as the Girl Scouts in our class said they were—all crunchy and gooey and chocolaty. Personally, I can't see why they're set aside special as an outdoor treat like it's a law. I plan to stick a marshmallow on a fork, roast it over a stove burner, then smash it and a Hershey's bar between two graham crackers any old time I feel like it.

After supper, we told ghost stories, which is a rule when you are on a camping trip. But when it was time for bed, Fancy seemed nervous. "Can I sleep in your tent, Mom?" she asked.

"I gave you a lantern," Mrs. Nelson said, putting her arm around Fancy's shoulder.

Fancy shook her head. "The battery won't last." Then she said to me, "You can sleep in the other tent with Miss LaRue. Is that okay?"

I was looking forward to all the giggling and goofing around stuff you see on TV sleepovers. "Sure," I said, disappointed. "That's okay."

The way Fancy was acting surprised me. But then I remembered all those night-lights in her bedroom.

And I realized with a shock that there *is* one thing Fancy is afraid of—the dark. That night there was no moon, so it was really black. Mama wasn't very generous with electricity, so dark didn't bother me at all. It was strange to think that, in this one thing, Mama's stinginess had made me braver than Fancy.

After we were settled in our sleeping bags, all I could concentrate on was Margo LaRue's cologne. Then my feelings turned on me and I thought of my mother's one luxury, her rose-scented soap. I hadn't told Mama that Margo LaRue was coming with us. And I didn't know I'd be sharing a tent with her as if I was her daughter. Then I heard her say, "Amelia, are you still awake?"

I didn't answer, just breathed in a slow and even rhythm like people do when they're sleeping.

She patted my head like she'd done a thousand times before. Then she whispered, "Sweet dreams, Amelia. Sleep tight."

I thought about what Miss Weinman said. How I filled the hole in Margo LaRue's heart like I was her daughter. But I wasn't her daughter. And I couldn't fill the hole in her heart because I had too many in my own. Then I thought of Mama, all alone with her *bad* heart, and I felt guilty.

"I have to go home," I said, in a panic so bad I could hardly take a breath.

"What's the matter?" Margo LaRue asked. "Are you sick?"

"No. I'm fine. I just have to tell my mother something."

I unzipped my sleeping bag and put on my sneakers.

"Well, wait a minute," Margo LaRue said. "I'll walk you home. It's too dark to go by yourself."

"That's okay," I said, and ran out of the tent as fast as I could.

When I got home, I stood by my mother's bed, breathed in the aroma of her rose-scented soap, then watched her sleep. I patted her head and said, "Sweet dreams, Mama. Sleep tight."

When I got into my own bed, the world felt right again. I thought about all the times I'd wished that Margo LaRue was my mother. And then I realized that sometimes what you wish for isn't what you want at all.

22

Love, Amelia

Dear Jack,

I'm saving your letters in a shoe box in the back of my closet. It is half full already because you are so long-winded. (Ha! Ha!) I'm glad about your new job at the mill and that you saved enough money to move out of the YMCA. Does your new rooming house have a pool like the Y did? Just kidding! Plus, now that you have your own telephone, maybe you can call me once in a while. Fancy said I can call you from her phone any time I want!

Most of this letter will be about school because that's almost all I'm doing right now, besides helping Margo LaRue. You might already know some of this stuff. I'm not sure how much has changed since you were there a hundred years ago. (Grin)

Junior high is where you get a second chance to

shine. It is much bigger than Sullivan's Falls Elementary, so there are lots of new kids to meet from other towns who didn't know you when you looked like a toad. The one lousy part is that they group the kids according to how smart they are. Naturally, Fancy is with the brains and I'm in the middle, so we don't have one single class together. Here is my schedule, so if you decide to think about me on any given day, you'll know where I am and what I'm doing.

8:30–8:45 Homeroom (Rm. 106) Miss Fern

Miss Fern is young and pretty and teaches English, which is my favorite subject. She has pierced ears and wears monogrammed sweater sets. (I think you two would make a cute couple.) I only get to have her while she takes attendance and reads the announcements. (That stinks!)

8:50–9:30 English (Rm. 214) Miss Livsey

I think Miss Livsey could be in *Ripley's Believe It or Not!* She has to be the oldest teacher in the entire world. (I asked her if she had you in seventh grade, but she couldn't remember. I don't think she remembers very much!) She has thin lavender hair and cloudy gray eyes. And there is a mystery odor attached to her that is hard to put your finger on. Kind of the way an attic smells. She wears those wide, black shoes that are made special for people whose feet have given up.

Mostly, Miss Livsey sits at her desk with a cup of tea and works a crossword puzzle while we write hundred-word compositions to go with titles like "What Makes Me Happy." (Does she think she is teaching second grade?) At the end of the class, she chooses a random person to read their paper out loud. One day she had us write about something scary. A boy named Randall Frost read, "There was a war." And then he finished with ninety-six *Bangs*! I don't think Miss Livsey heard him over the squealing from her hearing aid, because when he finished, she smiled and thanked him for reading his lovely story.

Since I really like English, you can imagine how disappointing this is. I just hope that next year I will get a teacher who still has a little something left.

9:35–10:15 Home Economics (Rm. 111) Mrs. Sample

Mrs. Sample calls us *ladies*, as if we are already grown-up married women. "Ladies, today we're going to learn the correct way to wash dishes." (I could teach them that!) "Ladies, you can make a whole week's worth of delicious meals from one good-size turkey." "*Ladies!* You *can't* talk and listen at the same time." She uses that last one a lot. You just know that she would love to scream, *"Shut the hell up!"* But I have a feeling she really needs her job. Plus, you can imagine how thrilled we were when she announced that our big project for the year will be to make a three-tiered skirt out of a bedsheet and then model it at the annual home ec fashion show in front of the whole school. I am going to be sick that day.

10:20–11:00 Math (Rm. 302) Mr. Dropp

Mr. Dropp always puts an impossible problem on the board to see if anybody in the class will surprise him and know the answer. This is what he had there this morning:

Solve for x

$y = 4$

$x + 3y = 14$

My brain said, *"What?"*

Mr. Dropp was standing at attention by the board, rolling a piece of chalk between his thumb and forefinger. His sandy-colored hair is cut drastic short, like if they called him to fill in for a drill sergeant, he would say, "Yes, sir! Ready for duty, sir!"

We have assigned seats, and I am in the middle of the front row, two feet away from Mr. Dropp's belt buckle. I think he puts the hopeless ones up front so we are forced to pay attention. I was examining a button on my sweater, trying to be invisible, but I could feel his eyes boring a hole into the top of my head. And sure enough, even though a couple of arms were waving around, he said, "Miss Rye, would you like to try this one?"

My face turned into a furnace as I watched him rest

his hand on my desk, drumming the first two fingers. "Well," he said, not mean. "How about it?"

I watched those fingers, and something in my brain clicked into gear. "Two?" The word slipped out, sounding as lily-livered as I felt. I waited for him to say, "Wrong, dummy!" Instead he said, "That's right, Miss Rye. Good."

As I watched his hand slide away from my desk, I had no idea what had just happened. Maybe he took pity on me because math is so difficult and he knows I am trying my best. But something tells me that Mr. Dropp's class won't be so bad after all.

11:05–11:45 Social Studies (Rm. 288) Mr. Fuentes

All I can say is *Yum! Yum! Yum!* Not *yum* social studies. I hate social studies. But I *love* Mr. Fuentes. All the girls love Mr. Fuentes. He is smack out of college, I think, and make-you-faint good-looking—the genuine tall, dark, and handsome type. The forward girls don't even pretend to hide the fact that they are flirting with him. You'd think the wedding ring he wears would count for something. I just think Mrs. Fuentes is one lucky woman.

11:50–12:10 Lunch

The first day, I sat at a table of kids that looked just as scared as I was. But now we all know each other, we're friendly even, so lunch is pretty okay, except for the food—they even ruin the peanut butter.

12:15–12:55 Science (Rm. 174) Mrs. Nelson

Fancy's mother is *the best* teacher in the world. Right now we are learning about digestion, which can be gross, but she even makes *that* interesting—how the different parts of the body know just what to do with the tuna fish sandwich I had for lunch. Of course, I don't let on to anyone that I spend more time at her house than I do at my own and that I even know what kind of toothpaste she uses.

1:00–1:40 Study Hall (Rm. 100) Monitor

I don't even know what Monitor's real name is. He's a huge, tough-looking guy who sits at a desk in a room with a hundred kids and reads a newspaper. Word around school is that he's a bouncer at Pappy's Bar on the weekends. He made it clear on the first day that he's not there to answer questions, so don't even try.

1:45–2:25 Gym, Music, Art

I have gym on Monday, Wednesday, and Friday. Most of the time we play dodgeball and try to wallop each other. I hate that game so much that I'm not going to say any more about it. Period.

Music is Tuesday. The teacher is nice, but the songs she chooses are pure lame. Mostly I just pretend to sing and watch the clock. She is all excited about the Christmas concert. I plan to be sick that day, too!

Art is on Thursday. Well, Jack, you'll probably be as surprised as I was. After I painted a still-life picture of flowers in a vase that the teacher had set up in the front of the room, she stood behind me and stared at it for a long time. Then she told me that I have real talent—*natural talent* is what she called it—that I was born with it. She says artists see things differently from ordinary people—like light and shadows—because their eyes are connected to their souls. And their innermost thoughts come out through their brushes. The kids in that class crane their necks to see what I'm going to come up with next. It is hard not to let a thing like that go to your head.

2:25 Dismissal (*Yay!*)

Now you know what my day is like. When you have a chance, send me your schedule so I'll know about yours, too.

I have to stop now because I want to get this letter to the mailbox on the corner before Mama comes home.

Write soon!

Love,

Amelia

P.S. Mama is taking me to Ogdensburg on the bus on Sunday to see Charlotte. Mama goes every month, but she's never brought me. Of course I want to meet my sister, but I'm not looking forward to going inside an insane asylum. I will write and tell you if they let me out. (Ha! Ha!)

23

Some things just plain stink!

Charlotte was sitting on a straight-back chair next to her bed at the far end of a huge ward. Almost everything in that room was white—walls, ceiling, rows of perfectly made beds. All that broke the starkness were the hardwood floor and the black bars across the windows like in our gym at school—and, of course, Charlotte. She was wearing a red dress with black plastic buttons—one missing—and high-top sneakers with no laces and no socks. She was only thirty-three, but she looked as old as Mama and just as sad.

"Here's my baby," Mama said as she ran her hand down Charlotte's cheek. When Mama kissed her, Charlotte pulled away, rocked back and forth, and moaned—low. "It's all right, darling," Mama said to her as she stroked Charlotte's hair. "Nobody's going to hurt you. Mama's here." And she kissed her again.

Then she motioned for me to come nearer. "This is your sister Amelia," Mama said, pulling me even closer. "I brought her with me this time so you could meet her."

"Hi," I said. But when I put out my hand to touch hers, Charlotte straightened and screamed—huge.

Fear grabbed me by the throat so hard that I couldn't breathe. Then I started to run and I didn't stop until I found the door we'd come in. I sat on the brick steps and tried to catch my breath. It was near noon and the sun was shining, but I was freezing. I folded my arms across my chest and rocked back and forth the same as Charlotte had. It seemed like hours before Mama came out, but when she did, she didn't yell at me like I thought she was going to. All she said was "Let's go. We don't want to miss the bus."

When I was settled in my seat, I thought about how gently Mama had treated Charlotte, and I realized that she really *did* know how to love a daughter—just not me. And I wondered what there was about that strange, sick woman with the dead eyes that made her my mother's golden child.

The bus was empty when the sound of a siren woke me up. I looked out the window and realized that I'd slept all the way home and that there was an ambulance pulling away from the station. The bus driver came down the aisle and stood next to me. "Where's my mother?" I asked him. "Did she go inside to use the restroom?"

His face was scary serious. "You'd better come with me," he said. "You can wait inside with Rita."

Before he left, the driver went to the counter and whispered something to the woman behind it. Then she walked over to me. "Your mother's been taken to the hospital," she said softly. "Is there someone I can call?"

When Margo LaRue came for me, I already knew in my soul that my mother was dead. "She died in her sleep," Margo said. "They think her heart finally gave out."

When most people hear news like that, they fall apart. But I didn't. I knew how weird I must have seemed, so I tried to cry, but nothing came.

"I'll take you home with me," Margo LaRue said as she led me out of the bus station. "You can sleep there tonight."

Then my heart started to wake up and I thought how Mama would feel if she knew I was going to sleep at Margo LaRue's apartment. "Maybe I could stay at Fancy's," I said. I didn't give a reason, just waited for her reaction.

"Well, sure, honey," she said, sweet. "If that's what you want. I know they'll be glad to have you."

The next day, Fancy and Mrs. Nelson stayed home from school and took me to the train depot to pick up

Jack. When we got home, he sat me down on the couch and put his arm around me. "I sure wish I knew what to say that would make you feel better," he said, giving me a little squeeze.

"I'm okay," I said. "It's kind of like I don't know *how* to feel." I looked into his eyes. "I'm pretty sure it's supposed to be worse than this, though."

"Same here," he said. "She was my mother, too, and it's as if I didn't even know her."

But Sylvia knew how to feel—*mad!* After Mrs. Nelson called Jack, he called the information operator and got hold of Sylvia. The minute she and Sam and William walked in the front door, she was on Jack good. "What are you doing here, anyway?" she yelled. "I thought you were in prison."

Jack stayed calm. "I was."

His cool riled up her storm. "I hope you don't think you're going to live here," Sylvia said. "Because this is *my* house now." She opened her purse and waved the paper Mama'd signed in Jack's face. "And I have the proof right here."

Jack shook his head. "I'm not going to live here. I just came for the funeral."

"Well you should leave before Daddy gets home. You disgraced the whole family, especially him."

When I heard that my daddy was on the way, my insides knotted up tight—with a huge zap of excitement thrown in.

"I know I disappointed everybody," Jack said. "And I'm sorry about that."

"*Sorry*'s not good enough," Sylvia barked. "You almost killed Mama and Daddy with the shame you heaped on them."

"I just came to be with Amelia," Jack said, flat. "As soon as the funeral's over, you'll never have to see me again."

As the two of them talked, William inched toward Jack until he was right next to him. "So *you're* the jailbird," William said, cocky. "Ma said you killed a guy."

"You must be William," Jack said, holding out his hand. "It's nice to meet you."

William pumped Jack's hand so hard you'd think he'd just met Jesse James. "Do you have your gun with you?" he asked, all excited.

Jack ignored William's question and turned to me. "Why don't we go over and break the bad news to Grandpa Thomas and let these folks get settled?"

"I want to go with Uncle Jack," William whined.

"You're not going anywhere with him," Sylvia said.

"But I want to—"

"I said *no!*" She pointed to a chair. "Now just go over there and sit down."

Wow, I thought. She *really* didn't want William to go with Jack. And I wondered what she'd have to promise her baby boy to get the pout off his face.

Sam had been standing by the door, and as he moved to let us by, he said, "Hey, Jack. Good to see ya."

"Great to see you again, too," Jack said.

As I passed Sam, he nodded to me and I nodded back, no nice talk.

"I don't like him," I said, after Jack had closed the door.

"Who? William?"

"No, not William. He's just strange."

"Sam?"

"Yeah."

"How come?" Jack laughed a little. "As far as I know, he's just strange, too."

"He stole Grandpa Thomas's watch."

Jack looked surprised. "Sam did?"

"Yup."

"Are you sure?"

"I saw him."

I told Jack the story, and afterward he just nodded. But there was a look on his face like the wheels in his head were turning fast.

Grandpa Thomas was lying in bed, staring out the window. Jack stood next to him and put his hand on his arm. I stood next to Jack and held Grandpa Thomas's hand.

"We came to tell you that Ma died yesterday," Jack said. "It was peaceful. She didn't suffer."

I watched for tears to come in Grandpa Thomas's eyes, but they didn't. They came in my eyes instead—first one and then a river. I think hearing Jack's words made the whole thing true.

Jack stayed dry-eyed, but he held me while I cried. When I was all washed out, we went back to Mama's house. The first thing Jack did was to ask Sam to step outside with him. I knew what he was up to. I went out on the porch and said, "Jack, is it okay if *I* do this?"

He smiled. "Sure. He's all yours."

As soon as Jack had gone inside, I looked Sam straight in the eye and said, "I want Grandpa Thomas's watch back."

Sam looked at me long and hard, as if I were a spider he'd like to squash. Then he glanced over at the living room window and saw Jack watching us. "Yeah, okay," he said. "You can have it back. It keeps lousy time anyway." I think he believed Sylvia's lies about Jack's killing a man, the same as William did, and he wasn't taking any chances. He slid the watch off his wrist and handed it to me. Then he smiled fake, as if we were having a good old time, and added, "I was only just borrowing it anyway."

"Sure you were," I said, snotty. I walked toward the door, and as I was turning the knob, I said, "The same way you're going to borrow Mama's house."

As soon as I'd given Jack a nod, he headed for the

kitchen. "I'll go whip us up something for supper," he said. "If everybody's settled in, just take it easy and I'll call you when it's ready."

Sylvia'd gotten her family settled all right. She had William set up in my room, and Sam's suitcase was near Grandpa Thomas's door. "You can sleep with me in Mama's bed, Amelia," she said, smothering me with a hug. "You need family with you at a time like this. And when I get you home to Maine, we'll share my bed like sisters do."

I smiled all phony sweet, but my insides turned sour. There was no way I was going to sleep with Sylvia in my dead mother's bed, and to get me to Maine, she'd have to drag me by my hair, and then I'd hitchhike right back to Grandpa Thomas. I'd sleep in the Shady Oaks parking lot if I had to. Just thinking about all that stuff made my head hurt, so I decided to go help Jack in the kitchen.

That night, I slept on the couch, and Jack slept on the floor next to me. I cried and told him about the paper Mama signed and how Sylvia thought she was going to take me home to Maine.

He reached up and held my hand. "Don't worry about that now," he said, low. "Just get some sleep. We'll figure out something."

Margo LaRue had Mama fixed up real special. She was wearing her good blue church dress that Jack had taken over to Jackson's Funeral Home. Her hair was all done up pretty, and she even had a hint of makeup on—just a little rose lipstick and rouge to match the inside velvet of the casket. The distressed look I was used to was gone, and her face looked peaceful—pleased, almost.

"She looks nice," I told Margo LaRue when she came to stand near me by the coffin.

Margo put her arm around me, smiled, and said, "She deserved that much." Then Margo left. She'd told me earlier that she wasn't going to stay for the funeral—that it wasn't her place to be there.

"Who was that woman?" Sylvia asked, after Margo LaRue was gone. Her eyes were suspicious.

"I don't know," I said. "She didn't tell me her name."

Then the organ record started and it was time to sit down for the funeral. My daddy hadn't come after all. I wondered if he *ever* would. Sylvia, Sam, William, Jack, and I sat in the front row. Judge Watson, Mrs. Nelson, and Fancy were right behind us. Miss Weinman and my sixth-grade teacher, Miss Annie Pine, were a few rows back, but the rest of the seats were empty, which made me sad. Not even one First Redeemer or A&P person showed up.

But then, just as the preacher was about to say his first words, my father walked in and sat right next to me. He looked just like his picture, only older. His coat smelled like fresh air, but when he took that off, the rest of him smelled like Aqua Velva—a lot of Aqua Velva.

Sylvia reached across me, touched his arm, and grinned. He nodded and smiled back, only his was the funeral type of smile, hardly there because it was a solemn time. And then he looked at me and whispered, "Do you know who I am?"

I nodded.

"I'm awful sorry about your mama and all," he said. His voice was kind. Just like I thought it would be. He put his arm around me, and I felt safe—like that was how it was supposed to be at your mother's funeral. For so long I'd had the dream that he'd come back, and now, my dream had finally come true.

When the preacher was talking about what a wonderful, loving person Mama was, Sylvia carried on something fierce—sobbing and sniffling and wiping her nose with wads of Kleenex she kept pulling from her purse. I guess she figured she ought to pretend to be sad since she was about to walk off with the deed to her dead mother's house.

After the service, Mrs. Nelson invited our family over for cake and coffee. When we finished eating, Judge Watson asked us to come into his den—he had something to discuss with us. "I thought you might want my help in settling Mrs. Rye's estate," he said when we were all sitting around a beautiful dark wood table. "I know this is a sad and confusing time for all of you."

"It's not confusing at all," Sylvia chirped, like she was the head canary at a bird festival. She opened her purse, took out the will Mama signed, then slid it toward Judge Watson. "It's all right there in black and white."

After he read it, he looked at Sylvia and said, "We have to make sure this is a legal document."

"Oh, it's legal, all right," Sam said. He grabbed the paper, held it up, and spanked it. "The old lady's signature is right there."

Then my daddy spoke up. "Actually, *I'd* planned on moving back to Sullivan's Falls to take care of my youngest daughter." He looked at me and smiled. "She needs me now." I guess he didn't realize how much I'd needed him all along. He must have thought that having Mama was enough. "And, of course," he added, "we'll have to have that house. The poor little thing couldn't live in the street."

Things were starting to look up, but then Sylvia spoke the words that slapped me out of my dream. She glared at Daddy and said, "Why, you no more want to take care of Amelia than a dog wants fleas. You just want the house because that woman in Iowa—your latest meal ticket—threw you out. Besides," Sylvia added, "I thought you were going to come live with us in Maine and we'd all care for Amelia and share the money from the house."

"What are you talking about?" Daddy snarled. "I'll take care of my own daughter in my own house. It's just that until now, her mother—may she rest in peace—wanted to raise her on her own."

What? I thought.

My father smiled across the table at me. "You did get the letters I sent you every week, didn't you, honey bunch?" Then he let the muscles in his face go limp, so his look changed to pathetic. "Or maybe your mama burned them so you wouldn't know how much I cared."

Things were really starting to stink. I didn't mention that it had been my job to bring in the mail for as far back as I could remember. I hadn't seen any letters from him.

I looked over at my father's phony sad face and thought about all those years I'd waited for him to rescue me. But then I realized that I'm a lot stronger than he'll ever be. He'll always be waiting for someone to rescue *him*. Plus, I think he did me a favor by staying away. I might have grown up to be just like him, and that's not something I'd ever want.

"I'd like to talk with Amelia alone, if you don't mind," Judge Watson said. "You can all go back into the dining room and help yourselves to more refreshments. I'll let you know when we're finished."

24

Love, Mama

Sometimes when you think you have a thing figured out just right in your head, real life butts in and switches everything around. The day my mama went to see Judge Watson, she had him draw up a new will—complete with a gold seal and red ribbons and everything. And that will left the house and a good-size bank account to me. I had no idea that Mama'd ever saved a penny in her life, but there was enough in that account to pay my expenses and send me to college with some left over. And she'd asked Judge Watson to help me choose a guardian until I was old enough to be on my own. That's when I realized that Mama really did love me. She just didn't know how to show it when she was alive.

On the day of the funeral, when Judge Watson had me to himself, he explained everything and then asked me about the guardian part. I thought I probably should choose Daddy because he was my own flesh-and-blood father. But then I thought about how he'd been missing all those years, and that the only reason he was hanging around was because I owned a house.

So I chose Jack. He didn't want anything—just a family—the same as me.

I stayed with Fancy while Jack went to Albany to get his things. When he came home, he landed a job at the paper mill, and now he's taking chef classes at the community college. He plans to open a fancy restaurant someday. He's going to call it Amelia's, which I think has a very nice ring to it.

I don't know if I'll ever see my daddy or Sylvia's family again because they were burning mad when they found out what Mama did. It's funny how a person can reach up out of the grave and get the last smack in.

I bet Sam and Sylvia will keep on living together and being miserable. I just wish William could get away from them. I don't think he's hopeless. He just got a raw deal in the parents department. And I'm sure my daddy will find another meal ticket. He's still kind of handsome, and there are a lot of women out there who will be mesmerized by his kaleidoscope blue eyes.

I'm still helping Margo LaRue at Shady Oaks—

because I like being there, not for money. But I've given up the Avon part. And I've paid her back in full for all the things she bought me.

Seventh grade is almost over, and believe it or not, I am cocaptain of the after-school field hockey team. And Fancy's talked me into joining the ski club next year, which I will do mostly because I love the outfits skiers get to wear, especially the stretch pants and the cute parkas.

The Mashers don't bother Fancy and me anymore. In fact, they don't bother anybody. They're too busy being bullied by the eighth-grade thugs. Sometimes people get what's coming to them!

Margo LaRue finally saved up enough money to buy a house. She chose a run-down one right across the street from mine and is fixing it up all cute with new aluminum siding, gray. I'm glad she's there in case I need some girlie advice. And more good news! She's dating the guy who put on her new roof. His name is Jim, and you can tell he really likes her. I think she finally found someone to fill the hole in her heart.

Right now, I'm on my way to visit Grandpa Thomas. I'm going to tell him about my new kitten and about the good time Fancy and I had last night when she slept over at my house and about the lasagna Jack made. Plus, there's this boy in school—

As I'm walking into Shady Oaks, I think how lucky I am to have Jack. But then I remember Fancy and

Mrs. Nelson and Judge Watson and Margo LaRue and I realize that I had a family all along. I just didn't know it.

And then I think about Mama and how I had her all wrong in my head. A lot of women whose lives had turned as sour as hers would have given up and farmed me out to anybody who'd take me. But she didn't. Even when she was completely worn out, she kept going to work so my future would be taken care of. And I bet I wasn't the only one who sat by the window at night watching for Daddy to come home. I just wish I'd figured this out sooner so she could know how I feel. But you know what? I bet we'll be reunited in heaven someday—even if I never do get baptized.

And I'll tell her then.

ACKNOWLEDGMENTS

Many thanks to my agent, Wendy Schmalz. She's smart and funny and I love her!

My amazing editors, Melanie Kroupa and her assistant, Sharon McBride, and Margaret Ferguson and her assistant, Beth Potter, worked tirelessly to transform a big messy pile of papers into a shiny new book. I'm grateful to all of them.

A big thank-you to Karla Reganold and Susan M. S. Brown, who patiently and thoughtfully copyedited my book. And to Robbin Gourley and Natalie Zanecchia for designing the snazzy jacket.

Betty DeGeneres always reads my stories first and makes me feel so good. Thank you, Betty.